The Vineyards of Calanetti
Saying "I do" under the Tuscan sun...

Deep in the Tuscan countryside nestles the picturesque village of Monte Calanetti. Famed for its world-renowned vineyards, the village is also home to the crumbling but beautiful Palazzo di Comparino. Empty for months, rumors of a new owner are spreading like wildfire...and that's before the village is chosen as the setting for the royal wedding of the year!

It's going to be a roller coaster of a year, but will wedding bells ring out in Monte Calanetti for anyone else?

Find out in this fabulously heartwarming, uplifting and thrillingly romantic new eight-book continuity from Harlequin Romance!

A Bride for the Italian Boss by Susan Meier

Return of the Italian Tycoon by Jennifer Faye

Reunited by a Baby Secret by Michelle Douglas

Soldier, Hero...Husband? by Cara Colter

His Lost-and-Found Bride by Scarlet Wilson

The Best Man & the Wedding Planner
by Teresa Carpenter

His Princess of Convenience by Rebecca Winters

**Saved by the CEO* by Barbara Wallace
Available February 2016**

Dear Reader,

When I was a little girl, I collected pictures of movie stars because my parents' best friends ran a movie theater in Roosevelt, Utah. They saved me posters and film release artwork. I fell in love with Grace Kelly and began getting more signed pictures from her. Years later when I traveled to Europe, I made a stop in Monaco to view the palace where she lived with Prince Rainier. I saw the video of their fabulous wedding. Talk about my fantasy! To marry a prince!

I must have dreamed that fantasy every time I watched *Cinderella* or *Sleeping Beauty*. What young girl hasn't? In the seventh book of The Vineyards of Calanetti, *His Princess of Convenience*, Christina is no different than any other girl. She'd love to be swept away in a fantasy like that, especially since she's never felt special or beautiful.

But unlike other girls, she actually did become friends with a *real prince*! And...she married him, but you'll have to read the story to find out *how* it happened and *what* happened after they said "I do."

Enjoy!

Rebecca Winters

His Princess of
Convenience

—

Rebecca Winters

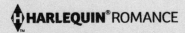

HARLEQUIN® ROMANCE

Recycling programs for this product may not exist in your area.

Special thanks and acknowledgment are given to Rebecca Winters for her contribution to The Vineyards of Calanetti series.

ISBN-13: 978-0-373-74368-1

His Princess of Convenience

First North American Publication 2016

Printed in U.S.A.

Rebecca Winters lives in Salt Lake City, Utah. With canyons and high alpine meadows full of wildflowers, she never runs out of places to explore. They, plus her favorite vacation spots in Europe, often end up as backgrounds for her romance novels, because writing is her passion, along with her family and church.

Rebecca loves to hear from readers. If you wish to email her, please visit her website at cleanromances.com.

Books by Rebecca Winters

Harlequin Romance

Greek Billionaires

The Millionaire's True Worth
A Wedding for the Greek Tycoon

The Greek's Tiny Miracle
At the Chateau for Christmas
Taming the French Tycoon
The Renegade Billionaire

Visit the Author Profile page
at Harlequin.com for more titles.

This book is dedicated to every woman who was once a little girl with a dream to be a princess.

CHAPTER ONE

August, Monte Calanetti, Italy

THE FLOOR-LENGTH MIRROR reflected a princess bride whose flowing white wedding dress, with the heavy intricate beading, followed the lines of her slender rounded figure to perfection. It probably weighed thirty pounds, but her five-foot-nine height helped her to carry it off with a regal air.

The delicate tiara with sapphires, the something-borrowed, something-blue gift from the queen, Christina's soon-to-be mother-in-law, held the lace mantilla made by the nuns. The lace overlying her red-gold hair, to the satin slippers on her feet, formed a whole that looked...pretty.

"I actually feel like a bride." Her breath caught. "That can't be me!" she whispered to herself. Her very recent makeover was nothing short of miraculous.

Christina Rose, soon-to-be bride of Crown Prince Antonio de L'Accardi of Halencia, turned to one side, then the other, as past memories of being called an ugly duckling, the chubby one, filled her mind.

From adolescence until the ripe old age of twenty-eight, she'd had to live with those unflattering remarks muttered by the people around her. Not that she really heard people say those things once she'd grown up and had been spending her time doing charity work on behalf of her prominent family. But she knew it was what people were thinking.

In truth her own parents were the ones who'd scarred her. They'd left her with nannies from the time she was born. And as she'd grown, her father had constantly belittled her with hurtful barbs by comparing her unfavorably to her friends. "Why is our daughter so dumpy?" she'd once heard him say. "Why didn't we get a boy?" They'd picked out the name Christopher, but had to change it to Christina when she was born.

His unkind remarks during those impressionable years had been wounds that struck deep, especially considering that Christina's mother had been a former supermodel.

Christina didn't know how her father could have said such cruel things to his daughter when she had loved both her parents so much and desperately wanted their approval. Between her unattractive brownish-red hair she'd always worn in a ponytail, to her teeth that had needed straightening, she'd been an embarrassment to her parents, who moved in the highest of political and social circles in Halencia.

In order to keep her out of sight, they'd sent their overweight daughter to boarding school in Montreux, Switzerland, where forty-five girls from affluent, titled families were sent from countries around the world.

Her pain at having to live away year after year until she turned eighteen had been her deepest sorrow. Christina was a poor reflection on her parents, whose world revolved around impressing other important people in the upper echelons of society, including the favor of the royal family of Halencia. Her father particularly didn't want her around when they were entertaining important dignitaries, which was most of the time.

If it hadn't been for Elena, the daughter of Halencia's royal family attending the French-speaking boarding school who'd become her closest friend, Christina didn't know how she would have survived her time there. With both of them being from Italian-speaking Halencia, their nationality and own dialect had immediately created a bond between the two women.

Though Elena bore the title of Princess Elena de L'Accardi, she'd never used it at school or behaved as if she were better than Christina. If anything, she was a free spirit, on the wild side, and good-looking like her older brother, the handsome Crown Prince Antonio de L'Accardi, who was the heartthrob of Halencia, beloved by the people. He'd had a hold on Christina's heart from the first moment she met him.

Elena never worried about breaking a few rules, like meeting a boyfriend at the local ice-skating rink in Montreux without their headmistress finding out. And worse, sneaking out to his nearby boarding school and going rowing on the lake at midnight, or sneaking her out for a joyride to Geneva in the Lamborghini his wealthy parents had bought him.

Christina had loved being with Elena and secretly wished she could be outgoing and confident like her dear friend. When the royal family went on their many vacations, Christina missed Elena terribly. It was during those times that Christina developed a close friendship with the quiet-spoken Marusha from Kenya.

Marusha was the daughter of the chief of the westernized Kikuyu tribe who'd sent his daughter to be educated in Switzerland. Marusha suffered from homesickness and she and Christina had comforted each other. Their long talks had prompted Christina to fly to Kenya after she turned eighteen and Marusha prevailed on her father to open doors for Christina to do charity work there.

Once she'd established a foundation in Halencia to deal with the business side, Christina stationed herself in Africa and lost herself in giving help to others. She knew she was better off being far away from home where she couldn't be hurt by her parents' dissatisfaction with her.

Caught up in those crippling thoughts,

Christina was startled to hear a knock on the door off the main hallway.

"Mi scusi," sounded a deep male voice she hadn't heard since his phone call two months ago. "I'm looking for Christina Rose. Is she in here?"

What was Antonio doing up here outside the doors of the bridal suite?

In a state of absolute panic, Christina ran behind the screen to hide. She'd come up here to be alone and make sure her wedding finery fit and looked right. For him to see her like this before the ceremony would be worse than bad luck!

Her heart pounded so hard she was afraid he could hear it through the doors. Trying to disguise her voice to a lower pitch, she said, "Christina isn't here, *signor.*"

"I think she is," he teased. "I think it's you playing a game with me."

Heat filled her cheeks. He'd found her out. "Well, you can't come in!"

"Now, *that's* the Christina I remember. Still modest and afraid of your own shadow. What a way to greet your intended beloved."

"Go away, Antonio. You should be at the chapel."

"Is that all you have to say after I've flown thousands of miles to be with my fiancée?"

The large four-carat diamond ring set in antique gold belonging to the L'Accardi royal family had been given to her at their engagement four years ago. Though she'd gone through the sham ritual for the most worthy reason, it had been a personal horror for Christina.

But when her parents had acted overjoyed that she'd snagged the crown prince, she felt she'd gotten their attention at last. Becoming a royal princess had made them look more favorably at her, and that had helped her enter into the final wedding preparations with growing excitement.

The minute Antonio had flown back to the States, she put the ring in a vault for safekeeping. To damage it out in Africa would be unthinkable. She'd only gotten it out to wear on the few times they were together in Halencia. Now it was hidden in her purse.

Christina had never felt like a fiancée, royal or otherwise. She knew Antonio had been dreading this union as much as she had, but he was too honorable for his own good.

Therefore Christina had to follow through on the bargain they'd made for Elena's sake.

"I didn't really believe this day would come."

He'd stayed away in San Francisco on business. The press followed his every move and knew he'd only been with her a handful of times since the engagement. He'd flown home long enough to be seen with her at the palace when she flew in from Africa. They came together in order to perpetuate the myth that they were in love and looking forward to their wedding day.

"San Francisco is a long way from Halencia, Christina, but I should have made time before."

"I know you've been married to your financial interests in Silicon Valley. No fiancée can compete with that." Not when she knew he'd been with beautiful women who were flattered by his attention and couldn't care less that he was engaged.

"You want to marry a successful husband, right? We had an agreement for Elena's sake."

He was right, of course, and it had been a secret between her and Antonio. But no one knew how Christina had pulled off such an improbable coup. The press had dubbed her the Cinderella Bride.

"I know, Antonio, and I plan to honor it. But not one second before I have to go downstairs to the chapel. Don't you have something else to do?"

"I'm doing it right now. Do you mind if I put a little gift on the bed for you?" He'd said it kindly. "I promise I won't look at you and I'll hurry back out."

"What gift? I don't want anything." She knew she sounded ungracious, but she couldn't help it. She'd never been so nervous in her life!

"It's your family brooch, the one that a Rose bride wears at her wedding to bring her marriage luck. One of the stones had come loose, so I had it repaired for you to wear and couldn't get it back to you until today."

The brooch?

Christina had heard the story behind the brooch all her life. It was supposed to bring luck, but she thought it had been lost a long time ago. She'd asked her wedding planner, Lindsay, to try and track it down for her, but to no avail. Her father's aunt Sofia certainly hadn't whispered a word about it during all the wedding preparations. Why hadn't she given it to Christina herself? Furthermore how did Antonio get hold of it?

"Thank you for bringing it to me," she said in a subdued voice. "It means a lot." In fact, more than he could know. A special talisman to bring her luck handed down in the Rose family. Now she felt ready.

"It was important to me that you have it. I want this day to be perfect for you."

She was thrilled by the gesture and heard the door open. If all he had to do was put it on the bed, she should be hearing the doors closing any second now.

"Are you still holding your breath waiting for me to go away, *bellissima*?"

Bellissima. Christina was not beautiful, but the way he said it made her feel beautiful, and today was her wedding day. She imagined he was trying to win her around with all the ways he knew how. She had no doubts he knew every one of them and more.

He laughed. "I'm still waiting, but we don't need to worry, Christina. After all, this isn't a real marriage."

She took a deep breath, realizing he was

teasing her. "Well, considering that this isn't going to be a real marriage, then I'd say we need all the luck we can get, so please leave before even the ceremony itself is jinxed by your presence here."

"A moment, *per favore*. It's a lovely bridal chamber. The balcony off this suite shows the whole walled village of Monte Cala-netti—it's very picturesque. I do believe you have a romantic heart to have chosen the Palazzo di Comparino for our wedding to take place. All nestled and secluded in this place amongst the vineyards rippling over the Tuscan countryside. I couldn't imagine a more perfect setting to celebrate our nuptials."

"After living near the vineyards of the Napa Valley in California all these years, I doubt a spot like this holds much enchantment for you. I guess I should be thanking you for letting our wedding take place here instead of the cathedral in Voti. Now, will you please go so I can finish getting ready?"

Christina was still her vulnerable self. Antonio stopped the teasing for a minute. "If it's any solace to you, I'm sorry for the position I've put you in."

After a long silence she said in a defeated tone, "Don't worry about it." He heard a sadness in her voice. "To be honest, it isn't as if I've had any other offers."

Her comment revealed a little of her conflict, the same conflict torturing him. There was a part of him that wanted to be crazy in love. If only he'd been an ordinary man like his best man, Zach, who could marry the woman who'd captured his heart. To choose a bride his heart wanted had never been a possibility.

When he thought about Christina, he realized she was having similar feelings that increased his guilt, but he couldn't dwell on that right now. It was too late for regrets. They would be married within the hour and he intended to be a good husband to her.

"Just remember we're doing this for Elena," he reminded her, hoping it would help her spirits. "She'll be up in a minute to escort you to the chapel." His eyes closed tightly for a moment. "Would it help if I told you I admire you more than any other woman I know?" It was the truth.

"Actually it wouldn't," she came back. "Thousands of women have entered into political unions disguised as marriage. We thought our engagement wouldn't last long. I thought that after four years you would fly to Africa and tell me in person we didn't have to go through with it."

"I'm afraid that wasn't our destiny, Christina. Everything has escalated out of control, the paparazzi have driven things to a higher pitch. Father's chief assistant, Guido, had me on the phone, urging me to marry you as soon as possible. The people are fed up with my parents. They want our marriage to take place for the good of the monarchy, reminding me of the danger of an abolished royal family if we wait."

"I know. That's because they want you for their king, and you need a queen. I understand that, but I'd rather you didn't start using meaningless platitudes with me."

"I was complimenting you," he asserted.

"I'm glad we could help preserve Elena's reputation along with your family's, but I don't want compliments. Your sister is doing much better these days and has a boyfriend who treats her well. Let's be happy for that and avoid any unnecessary pretense."

Antonio had come to the bridal suite already deeply immersed in troubled thoughts about their forthcoming marriage. Her last remark only added to his anxiety. He put the small velvet-lined box at the foot of the bed. After closing the doors quietly behind him, he left the bridal suite and walked down the corridor to the staircase of the three-storied palazzo.

Zach, his best friend, would be waiting for him in the bedroom just off the staircase of the second floor. By now some hundred and fifty guests had arrived for the ceremony, including his parents and their entourage. The small wedding Christina wanted had grown to royal proportions. It had been inevitable.

Antonio had met Christina when he went to Switzerland many times to visit his younger sister at boarding school. She always asked if her roommate, Christina, could come along with them when they went out for *fondue au fromage* or took the ferry to see the sights around Lake Geneva.

Though Antonio thought of Christina as his sister's pudgy friend, he'd found her sensible and soft-spoken, and probably the sweetest girl he'd ever met. That favorable impression of her grew deep roots when she'd phoned him in the middle of the night about Elena four years ago.

His sister had needed help because she and her loser addict boyfriend had been hauled off to jail on drug possession. Her boyfriend had been arrested and charged. What if Elena was next to be tainted with a jail record?

The paparazzi would have blown his sister's mistake into a royal scandal that would do great damage to the already damaged royal family. Antonio's parents hadn't been in favor with the country for a long time and were constantly being criticized in the press for their profligate ways.

In order to keep Elena's latest scandalous affair out of the news, Antonio had to think of something quick to take the onus off his wayward younger sister. Thankful beyond words for Christina's swift intervention with that phone call, he was able to turn things around and had talked her into entering into a mock engagement with him to create a new piece of news.

If the press focused on his stunning announcement, it would take up column space and deflect the paparazzi's interest in his sister's scandal, thus saving Elena's poor reputation and the family from further scrutiny and ruin.

After some persuasion Christina had agreed to fly to Halencia and become his fiancée because she loved Elena and had believed the engagement wouldn't last long. They'd be able to go their own separate ways at some future date. Or so Antonio had thought...

But once he'd leaked the news of their engagement to the press and it had gone public, everything changed. Elena's problems with the paparazzi went away like magic. Even more startling, the news of his engagement to the unknown Christina Rose grew legs.

The country approved of the Cinderella fiancée doing charity work in Kenya, whom he'd plucked out of obscurity. Immediately there was a demand for a royal wedding to become front and center. Guido was insistent on it happening immediately.

Antonio understood why. The royal approval ratings had dropped to an all-time low. In particular, his and Elena's philandering parents drew criticism with their string of affairs. There were accusations of them dipping into the royal coffers to fund their extravagant lifestyle. To his chagrin, Elena was also becoming infamous for her wild party ways and uncontrolled spending habits.

The press had been calling for the king and queen to step down. It was the will of the people that the monarchy be turned into a republic. Or…put Antonio on the throne.

A lot had gone wrong with his family while Antonio was pursuing his studies and business interests in the US. To his amazement, the separation that had distanced him from all this scandal had endeared him further to his subjects, who saw him as the one person to save the royal dynasty! Christina's hope that there wouldn't be a wedding was dashed. So was his… Guido's phone calls to him had changed everything.

And had made him feel trapped.

Once Antonio reached the second floor of the palazzo, he entered the bedroom designated as the groom's changing room.

"There you are!" Zach declared with relief. "You have a letter from your father." He handed him an envelope.

Antonio opened it and after reading it, he put the note back in the envelope and slid it in his trouser pocket. What were his parents up to now, spending the taxpayers' money on a honeymoon he hadn't asked for? He couldn't say no, but this was the last time public money would be spent on private, privileged citizens of the royal family.

"It's getting late," Zach reminded him. "You have to finish getting ready now. Lindsay has the wedding planned down to the second."

Antonio looked at his best man through veiled eyes. "I had to deliver the brooch to Christina so she could pin it on her wedding dress before the ceremony."

"How did that go?"

"She was hiding behind a screen and told me to leave." Considering the fact that she'd been forced to go through with this marriage they hadn't planned on, he shouldn't have been surprised she sounded so upset.

"That was wedding nerves. Christina was a sweetheart when Lindsay and I met with her for her fittings," Zach said, helping him on with the midnight blue royal dress uniform jacket.

After their unexpected exchange upstairs, Antonio didn't exactly agree with his friend. "She's not happy about this wedding going ahead."

Zach attached the royal blue sash over his left shoulder to his right hip, signaling his rank as crown prince. "She's a big girl, Antonio. No matter how much she cares for Elena, she wouldn't have agreed to an engagement with you if deep down she hadn't wanted to. Christina doesn't strike me as a woman who would bow out on a commitment once she'd given her word."

Antonio grimaced. "She wouldn't," he admitted, "but she would have had every right. When I was talking to her upstairs, I heard a mournful sound in her voice. She thought our engagement would have ended before now and she wouldn't have to go through with a real wedding." He'd felt her pain. From here on out he'd do everything he could to make her happy.

"You both underestimated the will of the people who want you to be their ruler."

His jaw hardened. "But she didn't ask for

this." He had a gut feeling there was trouble ahead.

"So use that genius brain of yours and look at your wedding as new territory. Think of it the way you do with every challenge you face at work. Think it and rethink it until it comes out right."

"Thanks for the advice, Zach."

His friend meant well, but Antonio couldn't treat it as he would a business problem. Christina wasn't a problem. She was a flesh-and-blood human being who'd sacrificed everything for her friend Elena. That kind of loyalty was so rare, Antonio was humbled by it. His concern was to be worthy of the woman whose selflessness had catapulted her to the highest rank in the kingdom.

Zach gazed at him with compassion. "Are you all right?"

He sucked in his breath. "I'm going to have to be. Because of you, I was able to give Christina that brooch. I can't thank you enough for getting it from Sofia."

"You know I'd do anything for you."

A knock on the outer door caused both

of them to look around. "Tonio—" his sister called out, using her nickname for him. "It's time. You should be out at the chapel."

"I know. I'll be right there."

"I hope you know how much I love you, brother dear."

"I love you too, Elena."

"Please be happy. You're marrying the sweetest girl in the whole world."

"You don't have to remind me of that." He'd put Christina on a pedestal since she agreed to their engagement. But he'd heard another side come out of her in the bridal suite.

"Lindsay says you two have to hurry!"

Zach's wife had planned this wedding down to the smallest detail. The schedule called for a four-thirty ceremony to avoid the heat of the day. He checked his watch. In the next fifteen minutes Christina would walk down the aisle and become his unhappy bride.

"We're coming," Zach answered for them.

Antonio glanced at Zach. "This is it."

"You look magnificent, Your Highness."

"I wish I felt magnificent. Let's go."

* * *

Christina heard Elena's tap on the door of the suite. "Come in."

Her friend hurried in, wearing a stunning blush-colored chiffon gown. On her stylishly cut dark blond hair she wore a tiara. "You look like the princess of every little girl's dreams," Christina cried softly.

"So do you. The tiara Mother gave you looks like it was made for you." Elena walked all the way around her, looking her up and down. "Guess what? This afternoon all eyes are going to be on you, *chère soeur.*" They would be sisters in a few minutes. Tears smarted Christina's eyes. "Oh, la-la, la-la," she said. "My brother will be speechless when he sees you at the altar. Your hair, it's like red gold."

"I just had some highlights put in."

"And you got your teeth straightened. How come you didn't do it a lot earlier in your life?"

"Probably reverse snobbery. Everyone thought I looked pathetic, so why not maintain the image? I knew it irked my parents. It upset me that they couldn't accept me for myself. But when the wedding date was announced, I realized I would have to be an ambassador of sorts.

"Antonio deserves the best, so I knew I had to do something about myself and dress the right way. Until a month ago, I never spent money on clothes. It seemed such an extravagance when there are so many people in the world who don't have enough to eat. Elegant high fashion wouldn't have changed the way I looked."

"Oh, Christina." Elena shook her head sadly. "I always thought you were pretty, but now you're an absolute knockout! If all the girls at our boarding school could see you, they'd eat their hearts out."

Christina's cheeks went hot with embarrassment. "Don't be silly."

"I'm being truthful. You've lost weight since the last time I saw you. Your figure is gorgeous. With your height, the kind I wish I had, that tiara gives you the elegance of a young queen. I'm not kidding. Lindsay found you the perfect gown and I love the interlocking hearts of your brooch. Is there anything more beautiful than diamonds?"

"It's been in the Rose family for years and supposed to bring luck. Antonio brought it to the room earlier. Do you think I pinned it in the right place?"

"It's right above your heart where it should be. You look as pure and perfect as I know you are."

She averted her eyes. "You know I'm not either of those things."

"I know how much your parents have hurt you, but you *can't* let that ruin your opinion of yourself. One day they'll realize you're the jewel in their crown. Today my brother is going to see you as his prize jewel. I've never told you this before, but all the time we were in Switzerland together, I had the secret hope he would end up marrying you one day."

I had the same hope, Christina admitted to herself, but she'd never confess it to anyone, not even Elena.

"The day I met you at school, you became the sister I never had and you never judged me. That has never changed. After we left school, our friendship has meant more to me than you will ever know."

"I feel the same," Christina said with a tremor in her voice.

"That awful night I phoned you when

Rolfe was arrested for drugs, I knew I could count on you to help me. I believe it's destiny you contacted Tonio. Now you're about to become his bride to save my reputation." Her eyes glistened with tears. "You have to promise me you'll be happy, Christina. Tonio's the best if you'll give him a chance."

Christina reached for Elena's hands. "I know he's the best because he was always kind to me when we were in Montreux. And because of his sacrifice for you, that takes brotherly love and goodness to a whole new level. He honors his family and his heritage. Who couldn't admire him?"

"But I want you to learn to *love* him!" Her eyes begged.

"You're talking a different kind of love." After he'd phoned to tell her the date they were going to be married, she was forced to accept her fate. "I haven't dated much, Elena. I did spend time with one doctor in Africa. But when I got engaged to Antonio, that ended any possibility of a relationship with him or any man, let alone potential love."

In a way, her engagement had helped her to hide from love for fear that she would never be good enough for anyone. If she wasn't good enough for her parents, why would she be good enough for any man?

Still, her parents had been overjoyed with the engagement, which made her happy. And Christina had adored Antonio in secret for years, not only for the way he loved Elena, but for his hard-work ethic. In Christina's new position as his wife, the number of people she'd be able to help with her charities would be vastly increased. Was it worth giving up on the possibility of true love?

Christina had never felt worthy of love and so had never been hopeful of meeting "the one." At the end of the day she'd reconciled herself to this marriage.

"Can you honestly tell me you're not excited about your wedding night?"

"Oh, Elena—you're such a romantic and I know you feel guilty about what's happening, but don't let that worry you. Yes, I'm excited, but mostly I'm nervous. Antonio and I have never spent time alone together. You know what I mean. But Antonio has been with other women both before and probably after our engagement. My eyes are wide-open where he is concerned. After the women he has been with, I'm afraid I'm not going to compare."

A stricken look entered Elena's eyes. "Don't you dare say that! And don't think about any of his past relationships. He knew they would never amount to anything, and today he's marrying *you*."

"I know, but it's still hard to believe." Christina stared at her friend. "I wasn't convinced Antonio planned to go through with our nuptials. You can't imagine my surprise when he finally called me and said I needed to start making the wedding plans with Lindsay."

"He meant it, Christina. I know he got engaged to you to save my skin, but he could have chosen any number of eligible royal hopefuls. Why do *you* think he chose you?"

"I was...convenient."

"That's not the answer and you know it. There was something deeper inside that drove him to choose you. I think you need to think about that as you walk down the aisle toward him today looking like any man's dream. If you don't believe me, take one more look in the mirror."

"You're very sweet."

"It's true. Tonio came to Switzerland a lot during our days at boarding school. He liked you right off and enjoyed your company. He trusts you."

"But he's not in love with me."

"Give him a chance and he *will* fall in love with you. *I've* always loved you and feel all the more indebted to you for the sacrifice *you're* making to save me and our family from scandal. Will you promise me one thing?"

"If I can."

"Pretend that today you're going to get married to the man you've always loved and who has always loved you."

I have always loved him...from a distance. There was no pretense on Christina's part.

Elena rushed over to her and they hugged.

"What's wrong, Elena? Are those tears?"

"I just don't want anything to go wrong. This wedding is all my fault. I'll pray for you and Antonio to be happy."

Christina took a big breath, sensing that deep down Elena was really worried. Why? What wasn't she telling her, unless her guilt was working overtime?

"It'll be fine, Elena." She'd made up her

mind about that. Today was her wedding day and she was living her fantasy of marrying the prince of her dreams. For once in her life she planned to enjoy herself. She could do it. She'd seen herself in the mirror and felt confident to be his bride.

"You'd better start working on it right now," Elena warned. "Otherwise you're going to give everyone a heart attack if you don't make an appearance in the chapel in the next minute."

"I'm ready."

"I love you, Christina."

"The feeling's mutual. You have to know that by now."

Elena blew her a kiss. "I do."

Together they walked down the stairs to the foyer of the palazzo and out the main entrance to the courtyard. The chapel faced the palazzo across the way with a beautiful fountain in the center. Lindsay was waiting for them inside the church doors of the foyer with their flowers.

She let out a gasp when she saw Christina. "You're perfect! Better than anything I'd imagined. So perfect, in fact, I can't believe my eyes."

Christina smiled at Zach's wife. "You out-did yourself, Lindsay. All the credit goes to you. This dress is divine."

Louisa, the owner of the palazzo, hurried toward her. "You're the most stunning bride I've ever seen."

"Thank you, Louisa. You look lovely too. I'm indebted to you for your generosity in letting us be married here. The Palazzo di Comparino is the most ideal setting for a wedding in all of Tuscany."

"It's been an honor for me. I told Prince Antonio the same thing."

Louisa had given Christina a tour of the newly renovated chapel yesterday. She'd met the elderly priest who would be marrying them. While he walked with her in private, they chatted about the renovations.

She'd been utterly enchanted with the fabulous unearthed fresco of the Madonna and child now protected by glass. The charming chapel had an intimacy and spiritual essence. It thrilled her to know she'd be taking her vows in here. She intended to make this the perfect wedding day.

"Everyone is inside waiting," Lindsay whispered. "Here's your bouquet, Christina."

"Oh—these white roses are exquisite."

"Just like you. And here's your bouquet, Elena." Lindsay had matched the flowers to the soft blush of her gown. "Zach will hand you the ring to give Antonio when the time comes during the ceremony. As we rehearsed, once you hear the organ, you and your father will enter the chapel with Elena five paces behind you. The king and queen are seated on the right side with their retinue. Your family and friends are on the left."

Christina looked around. "Where's my father?"

"I'm right behind you."

As she turned, her heart thudded mostly in fear in case she saw rejection in his dark gray eyes. He had a patrician, distinguished aura and was immaculately dressed. His gaze studied her features for a moment. "I'm glad to see you've changed for the better. Today the Rose family can be proud of you."

"You look very handsome too, Father."

"Christina?" Lindsay reminded her. "Take your father's arm."

The organist had started playing Wagner's "Wedding March." There'd probably never been this many people inside. Her joy was almost full.

She clung to her father as they slowly made their way down the aisle of the ornate interior. The only eyes she searched for were her mother's, wanting her approbation. Her mother, who was in her midfifties, was still a beautiful brunette woman and the envy of many.

Just once Christina hoped to find a loving smile meant for her alone. As she passed the pew, she made eye contact with her. A proud smile broke out on her mother's perfectly made-up face. That acknowledgment made Christina feel as if she were floating as she walked toward her prince.

She focused her attention on the two men standing at the altar before the priest. Zach, as best man, stood several inches taller than the crown prince, who was six foot one, according to Elena. They were watching her progress.

A slight gasp escaped her lips when she looked into the startling blue eyes of the man she was about to pledge her life to. It had been several months since the last time she saw him at the palace. His visit had been brief.

In full dark blue ceremonial dress, Antonio looked so splendid she was shaken by her reaction to him. His light brown hair, smart and thick, was tipped with highlights from the sun, reflecting a healthy sheen. With such a lean, fit body, he was the epitome of a royal prince every little girl dreamed of marrying one day.

How incredible that Christina was about to become his wife. *If I were the type, I'd pass out at the feet of the most desirable man in all Halencia. But I'm not going to make any mistakes today. This is my wedding day. I love it already.*

Caught up in all the wedding preparations, she felt that she *was* his beautiful bride and she intended to be the woman he was excited to marry. Her teenage dream had come true. The only thing more she could ask of this day was that the fantasy would last forever.

CHAPTER TWO

Maybe Antonio's eyes were playing tricks on him. The stunning woman walking on the arm of her father with the grace of a queen had to be Christina, but it was a Christina he'd never seen or imagined.

When did the brownish-red hair, which he remembered she'd worn in a ponytail, turn out to be a spun red gold?

Had her body ever looked like an hourglass before now?

The lace veil against her smooth olive skin provided a foil for her finely arched dark eyebrows. Because of the light coming through the stained glass windows, her crystalline gray eyes had taken on a silvery cast. Her red mouth had a passionate flare he'd never even noticed.

His gaze fell lower to the brooch she'd

pinned to the beaded bodice of her wedding
dress. The diamonds sparkled in the light
with every breath she took.

Elena approached her side to take the bouquet from her. When Christina smiled at his
sister, Antonio caught its full effect and was
blindsided by the change in her.

While he'd been talking to her earlier in
the bridal suite, parts of her sounded like the
woman he'd gotten engaged to four years
ago. But she wasn't the same person on the
outside. It threw him so completely that he
felt a nudge from Zach to pay attention to
the priest.

"Your Highness?" he whispered. "If you
will take your bride-to-be by the hand."

Antonio reached for her right hand. Her
cool, dry grip was decisive. If she was suffering wedding nerves, it didn't show. He
didn't know if he was disappointed by her
demeanor, which seemed unflappable.

In a voice loud enough to fill the interior, the priest began. "Welcome, all of you.
Today we are gathered here for one of the
happiest occasions in all human life, to celebrate before God the marriage of a man
and woman who love each other. Marriage

is a most honorable estate, created and instituted by God, signifying unto us the mystical union that also exists between Christ and the Church. So too may this marriage be adorned by true and abiding love. Let us pray."

Antonio bowed his head, but his burden of guilt over compelling Christina to follow through with this marriage weighed heavily on him. As Zach had reminded him, she'd entered into this union of her own free will because of her love for Elena, but the words *may this marriage be adorned by true and abiding love* pierced him to the core of his being.

In the past four years he'd done nothing to show her love. The only thing true about this marriage was their love for Elena, and on his part the need to preserve the monarchy. But at this moment Antonio made up his mind that their love for his sister would be the foundation upon which they built a life together.

Antonio's absence from her life except for those four quick visits had made certain she had no anticipation of love to come. To his surprise she sounded happy as she repeated the marriage covenant. He hadn't expected that.

When it was his turn to recite his vows, he felt the deep solemnity of the moment and said them with fervency.

"Who holds the rings?"

"I do," Zach responded.

"Grant that the love which the bride and groom have for each other now may always be an eternal round. Antonio? Take the ring and put it on Christina's finger saying, 'With this ring, I thee wed.'"

She presented her left hand while he repeated the words. Her hand trembled a little as he slid the wedding band next to the diamond from the royal family treasury he'd given her four years earlier. So she wasn't quite as composed as he'd thought, but it didn't make him feel any better. If anything, he felt worse because he'd done nothing to ease her into this union and lamented his selfishness.

Now it was her turn to present him with his ring. She took it and placed it on Antonio's finger. His new bride was suddenly so composed that again he marveled. "With this ring, I thee wed," she said in a steady voice.

They were married.

The deed was done.

"Antonio and Christina, as the two of you have joined this marriage uniting as husband and wife, and as you this day affirm your faith and love for each other, I would ask that you always remember to cherish each other as special and unique individuals, that you respect the thoughts, ideas and suggestions of one another.

"Be able to forgive, do not hold grudges, and live each day that you may share it together. From this day forward you shall be each other's home, comfort and refuge, your marriage strengthened by your love and respect."

Antonio's shame increased. *I've shown her no respect.*

"You may now kiss your bride."

When Antonio turned to her, he saw a look of consternation in her eyes. *Oh, Christina. What have I done to you? You're so good. So sweet.* His eyes focused on her lovely mouth before he grasped her upper arms gently and kissed her.

Not only her lips but her whole body trembled. Her fragrance assailed him. He deepened the kiss, wanting her to know he planned to make their marriage work. Whether she was putting on a show for everyone, or responding instinctively to new emotions bombarding her as they were him, he didn't know. But she kissed him back and he found himself wanting it to go on and on.

The priest cleared his throat, prompting Antonio to lift his mouth from hers. A subtle blush had entered her cheeks. He removed his hands.

"Antonio and Christina, if you'll turn around." When they'd done his bidding, he said in a loud voice, "May I present Crown Prince Antonio de L'Accardi and his royal bride, Princess Christina Rose. Allow them to walk down the aisle to the foyer of the chapel, where you can mingle outside."

Elena came forward to give Christina her bouquet, and then the organist played the wedding march. Taking a deep breath, Antonio grasped her free hand, still feeling the tingly effect of her warm, generous mouth on his. He guided her to the first pew where his parents were seated and stopped long enough for both of them to bow to the king and queen of Halencia.

To show Christina's parents his respect, he escorted her across the aisle to their pew to acknowledge them. He gave her a sideward glance. Her eyes glistened with unshed tears. He didn't know what that was about.

How could you know when you haven't spent any real time getting to know her?

More upset with himself and even more shaken by their kiss, he walked her slowly down the aisle. He darted her another glance, but this time she was smiling at everyone. She was so gracious it impressed the hell out of him. She could have been born to royalty.

He'd honored Christina's wishes by letting her plan the wedding here instead of the fourteenth-century cathedral in Voti. She'd insisted on a simple ceremony. If there'd been any royal formality or long traditional ceremony, she wouldn't have agreed. Antonio had been so thankful she hadn't backed out that he'd fallen in with her every wish.

In private he'd asked his parents to take a backseat so this could be Christina's day. She was beloved of the people, but she couldn't have abided all the pomp and circumstance. Since his parents were resigned to their fate to put Antonio on the throne, they'd acceded to his wishes. He'd even heard them say they were relishing the idea of retirement and looking forward to more freedom in the future.

At his engagement four years ago, Antonio had vowed to sacrifice his personal freedom and return from California to take the throne at a later date with Christina at his side. He'd felt a strong loyalty to his country and had always been conscious of his royal duty. But he'd only been prepared to marry her on *his* terms, and hadn't considered her fears.

There were going to be a lot of changes after his coronation in another week. He had a raft of constitutional issues that would put the royal family in a figurehead role, with specific duties. There would be a much reduced civil list, no hangers-on supported by the state; all personal belongings and lifestyle choices and holidays would be paid for by personal business interests rather than the state.

The areas of change went on and on, which was why the monarchy had been on the brink of disaster. This marriage would hopefully turn the tide of criticism. Christina's values of hard work and true charity resonated with the people. Her example of selflessness was the big reason they'd embraced Antonio as their soon-to-be king. Antonio still had to prove himself equal to the task. And much more, like becoming the husband Christina deserved.

He walked her outside and across the courtyard to the terrace bedecked in flowers at the side of the palazzo. A small orchestra was playing a waltz at one end of the terrace with an area reserved for dancing. Hundreds of tiny lights strewn among the trees and flowers made it look like a true fairyland and had created a heavenly fragrance. The grand serving table with its fountain and flowers was surrounded by exquisitely set tables, an enchanting sight he'd always remember.

The late-afternoon Tuscan sunshine shone down on them. The picturesque setting and vineyard had an indescribable beauty, yet all he could see for the moment was the stunning bride draped in alençon lace, still clinging to his hand. Antonio swallowed hard.

She's my wife! She's the woman I promised to love and cherish.

Suddenly he seemed to see a whole new world ahead of them, uncharted as yet. Her faith in their marriage made him open his eyes to new possibilities. This was their wedding day. He wanted it to be wonderful for both of them. After their kiss at the altar, he was eager to feel her in his arms.

"Christina? Look this way."

She was so dazed by what had happened at the end of the ceremony that she was hardly aware of the photographers brought in to make a record of their wedding day. When Antonio had deepened their kiss, she felt a charge of energy run through her body like a current of electricity. She could still feel his compelling mouth on hers.

Maybe this was how every bride felt when kissed on her wedding day. But Antonio wasn't just any man. He was her husband, for better or worse.

Before everyone could crowd around to congratulate them, Antonio pulled her close. "Do you mind if we talk to our guests later? I'd like to dance with you first," he said in his deep voice.

Her heart thumped hard before she looked at him. "I'd love it."

His hot blue eyes played over her features. "Let me put your bouquet on this table."

After he laid it down, Christina felt his arm go around her waist. The contact reminded her of the kiss they'd shared at the altar. She hadn't been the same since and was more aware of him than ever as he led her to the dance area.

She couldn't help thinking back to the time she'd been at boarding school. Never in her wildest imagination would she have believed she'd eventually become the wife of Elena's dashing older brother. This moment was surreal.

As he drew her into his arms she said, "You need to know I haven't done much dancing in my life."

He held her closer. "Didn't they teach you to dance at boarding school?"

"Are you kidding? Whatever you think goes on at boarding school simply doesn't happen. We were all a bunch of girls who'd rather be home. We all had a case of homesickness and waited for the letters that didn't arrive. We ate, studied and slept four to a room in an old freezing-cold chateau. You don't even want to know how frigid the water closet could be."

He laughed out loud, causing everyone to look at them.

"Once a week we were allowed to go to town with the chaperone. She chose the places we could visit. Elena managed to scout out the dancing places we weren't supposed to visit, then dragged me with her where we met guys who flocked around her."

"Sounds like my sister."

"She taught me the meaning of *fun*. The rest of the time we went to a symphony or an opera, and other times we went to a play, always on a bus. I liked the plays, especially one adapted from Colette's writings about a dog and cat."

Antonio started moving them around the terrace decorated with urns of flowers. "Tell me about them," he whispered against her hot cheek. His warm breath sent little tingles of delight through her body.

"Elena and I bought the books and studied the lines to help us with our French. Both animals loved their master and mistress. Their battles were outrageous and hilarious."

"You'll have to lend me the book to read."

"Anytime. Wouldn't it be fun if animals really could talk? I used to love the *Doctor Doolittle* books as a child. When I first got to Africa, I thought I really had arrived in Jollijinki Land."

He lips twitched and he held her a little tighter, but her gown provided a natural buffer. "I have a feeling you could entertain me forever."

She moved her head so she could look into his eyes. Marrying Antonio felt right. She felt like a princess. The feeling was magical. She was living her fantasy and never wanted it to end. Her parents were proud of her today. Everything was getting better with them. "This is a new experience for both of us, Antonio. Forever sounds like a long time. Let's just take it one step at a time."

His lips brushed hers unexpectedly, creating havoc with her emotions. "One step at a time it is. Since everyone is watching us, let's put on a show, shall we?"

She smiled at him. "I thought we'd already been doing that."

"They haven't seen anything yet."

Her adrenaline gushed as he waltzed them around the terrace. It didn't surprise her that he knew what he was doing. She followed his lead as he dipped her several times, causing people to clap. Dancing with him like this was a heady experience she hadn't anticipated. He must have been enjoying it too, because one dance turned into another.

"This is fun," he murmured against her lips. "Your idea for having our wedding here at the palazzo has turned out to be sensational. I remember once when the three of us climbed into the mountains above the vineyards lining Lake Geneva and came to an old farmhouse that had been turned into a quaint inn.

"You said it was your favorite place and went there often on your hikes and bicycle rides with Elena for fondue bourguignonne. I think you must have had it in mind when you chose the Palazzo di Comparino for our wedding. I see similarities."

Her head tilted back in surprise. "I can't believe you remembered that hike, let alone made the association with this place."

His gaze played over her features. "I've remembered all our outings. The truth is, I found you and my sister more entertaining than most of my friends, with the exception of Zach." His comment made her smile.

"When I did fly to Switzerland, I came because I wanted to. Being with you two was like taking a breath of fresh air and kept me grounded. I've never told you this, but I was always relieved to know you were there to help temper my sister. She's always had trouble with boundaries."

"And I was the insipid, boring tagalong, afraid to break out of my shell, right?"

He frowned. When he did that, he looked older and quite fierce. "You were shy, but amazingly kind to my sister. Even when she got herself into impossible situations you never judged her."

"You were kind to me too by including me. Remember the day we visited the Chateau de Chillon? We'd climbed up on the ramparts and I was taking a picture when I dropped my camera by mistake and it fell into the lake several hundred feet below."

"You should have seen the tragic look on your face," he teased.

"I was so upset, but you turned everything around when you bought me a new one just like it and gave it to me before you left us at the school." She felt her eyes smart. "That was the kindest thing anyone had ever done for me."

"Then we're even because Elena needed a constant friend like you and you were there for her in her darkest hours. You have no idea what that meant to me. I knew I could always count on you. I wish I could say the same for our parents. They've been so caught up in a lifestyle that has cost them the confidence of the people that they've neglected Elena, who needed a strong hand."

Christina sucked in her breath. "I needed her friendship too."

"Elena told me you had problems with your parents."

"Yes, but I don't want to talk about them right now. We were talking about your sister. She's so sweet. Elena cared about me when no one else did. She made me believe in myself."

"The two of you have an unbreakable bond. Otherwise you wouldn't have stayed close over all these years. You don't know how lucky you are. How rare that is."

"According to Elena, you have that kind of relationship with Zach."

He nodded. "But I didn't have a friend like you while I was at boarding school and college. It wasn't until I moved to San Francisco. If you want to know a secret, I envied you and Elena."

She heard a loneliness in his admission that went deep. "Because you're the prince, it was probably hard for you to confide in someone else during those early years. With you being expected to rule one day, you had to watch every step."

Antonio stopped dancing and grasped her hands in both of his. "You understand so much about me, Christina." His blue eyes had darkened with emotion. "But you paid a price by agreeing to get engaged to me."

Giddy with happiness she said, "What price is that when I'm having the wedding of my dreams?"

Her thoughts flew back to their engagement. The king and queen had thrown the supposedly happy couple a huge, glossy engagement party, but it had been the worst night of Christina's life. To have to be on show, self-consciously standing next to the most gorgeous man she'd ever known, she'd never felt so unglamorous in her life. Especially when she knew her parents considered her a failure.

Yet they'd acted thrilled over the engagement and made such a fuss over her that it made her happy that they showed her that kind of attention. She'd been starved for it. But once she saw the photos, she'd been unable to bear the sight of herself looking so dull and plump. But that was a long time ago and she refused to dwell on it.

The guests had been going through the buffet line before finding their seats at individual linen-covered tables with baskets of creamy roses and sunflowers. Christina had to admit the estate and grounds looked beautiful. A fountain modeled after the one in the courtyard of a draped nymph holding a shell formed the centerpiece. Everything looked right out of a dreamworld, including the beautifully dressed people.

Antonio drew her even closer as they walked past the guests to get their food. He handed her a plate and they moved back and forth, choosing a delicious tidbit here and there. But she was too happy and stimulated to sit down to a big meal with him at a table reserved for them alone.

Several of the guests had started to dance. Among them Louisa, who was being partnered by Nico. According to Louisa, the two of them weren't on the best of terms, but the way he was looking at her right now, Christina got the feeling they had a strong attraction. Well, well. It appeared the festive party mood had infected everyone.

Antonio finished what was on his plate. Since hers was empty, he put them both on the table. When he looked at her she was filled with strong emotion and said, "Today I'm so happy to be your wife, Antonio. I mean that with all my heart."

"Christina," he said in a husky voice, squeezing her hand. "Because of your sacrifice for me—for the country—I trust you with my life." He said it like a vow and kissed her fingers in a gesture so intimate in front of the wedding guests that she made up her mind to be the best wife possible.

Just then Louisa happened to pass by her. "You look radiant," she whispered.

Christina was still reacting to Antonio's

gesture as well as his words. "So did you out there dancing with Nico."

"Who knew he could waltz?"

Her comment made Christina chuckle. Antonio smiled at her. "I want to dance the whole evening away with you, but I think we need to say something to our parents."

They walked hand in hand toward the king and queen and they all chatted for a moment. Christina's parents were seated by them. While Antonio was still talking with his parents for a minute, her mother, dressed in an oyster silk suit, got up from the table to greet Christina with a peck on the cheek.

Though Christina had known this began as a publicity stunt, she'd tried to win her parents' affection. Four years later she was still trying and had hopes that her marriage to the future king had softened their opinion of her.

Her mother stared into her eyes. "You look lovely, Christina. I do believe that tint on your hair was the right shade."

A compliment from her mother meant everything. "I'm glad you like it."

"It's a good thing Lindsay planned everything else, including your new royal wardrobe. You'll always want to look perfect for Antonio."

"I plan to try."

"I know you will. Certainly today you've succeeded." Her voice halted for a minute before she added, "You've never looked so attractive."

Christina's eyes moistened. She couldn't believe her mother was actually paying her another compliment. In fact, she sensed her mother wanted to say more but held back.

"*Grazie*, Mama," she said in a tremulous voice, and kissed her mother's cheek.

Marusha stood nearby. Christina hugged her. She'd flown in for the wedding. Her family would be coming for the coronation. For this ceremony, only their closest friends and relatives made up the intimate gathering.

Next came Christina's great-aunt Sofia. "You look enchanting." The older woman embraced her. "Working in Africa has made all the difference in you," she said quietly. "You have a queenly aura that comes naturally to you."

Christina craved her aunt's warmth and hugged her extra hard. "I'm thrilled to be wearing the brooch." She was glad Antonio had sneaked up to the bridal chamber to give it to her.

"It suits you. I'm so proud of you I could burst."

"Don't do that!" she said as they broke into gentle laughter.

"I've been watching your handsome husband. He's hardly taken his eyes off you since we came outside." Her brown gaze conveyed her sincerity. "I can see why. You're a vision, and you're going to help Prince Antonio transform our country into its former glory. I feel it in these old bones. I have the suspicion that you didn't need the brooch to bring you good luck. You and your prince are special, you know?"

No, Christina *didn't* know, but she loved her aunt for saying so. "I love you."

Her great-aunt kissed her on the cheek before Elena rushed in to hug her hard. "Ooh— you're the most gorgeous bride I ever saw. I do believe you've knocked the socks off Tonio. All the time he's been talking to the parents, he's had his eye on you."

Sofia had said the same thing. From the mouths of two witnesses...

"The two of you looked so happy out there

it seemed like you were sharing some great secret. By the way, in passing I heard your mother tell your aunt Sofia that she'd never been so proud of you."

"Thank you for telling me. Things seem to be better with Mother," she whispered. "It is a beautiful wedding, isn't it?"

"It's fabulous, and you know why? Because you're Tonio's wife and will make him a better man than he already is. Meeting you was the best thing that ever happened to me. He's going to feel the same way once he gets to really know you the way I do."

Tears glistened on Christina's eyelashes. She hugged her again. "We're true sisters now," she whispered.

CHAPTER THREE

"Your Highness, the photographer is waiting for you and your bride to cut the wedding cake."

Antonio switched his gaze to Zach, but his mind and thoughts had been concentrated on Christina and it took a moment for him to get back to the present. "Thanks, Zach. We're coming."

"I hope you love wedding cake," she whispered as they made their way to the round table holding the fabulous three-tiered cake.

He flashed her a quick smile. "Is this the moment you're going to get your revenge on me for past misdeeds?"

"If you're referring to the chocolate you fed me full of cherry cordial that dripped down my blouse on one of our outings, I wouldn't be surprised." The impish look in her beautiful gray eyes was so unexpected that his heart skipped a beat.

"Be gentle," he begged, putting his arms around her from behind to help her make the first cut with the knife. Another chuckle escaped her lips. With great care she picked up the first piece and turned to him, waving it in the air as if trying to decide how to feed it to him. This produced laughter from the guests.

"Just take your best shot, whatever you have in mind."

"So I *do* have you a little bit worried."

"Please, Christina."

"I tell you what. I'll have a napkin ready." She plucked one off the table. "Now open sesame."

He closed his eyes and obeyed her command.

"You have to keep your eyes open, coward," she said in a low teasing voice.

"I can't do both," he teased back.

"Then I'll eat it instead."

Shocked by her response, he opened his eyes only to be fed the cake, part of which fell onto his chin into the napkin she held for him. The wedding guests laughed and clapped their hands. Of course everything had been caught by the videographer.

Christina cleaned him up nicely, then kissed his chin. "Thanks for being a good sport, Your Highness."

"Don't call me that."

She looked surprised. "No?"

"Not ever."

She flashed him a smile. "Are we having our first fight?"

Her question caught him off guard. Before he could respond, Lindsay came up to Christina with her bridal bouquet. "When you're ready to leave the party, you can toss it behind you."

"Thank you, Lindsay. All your planning has made this the most beautiful wedding party in the world. I've never been happier."

"You look radiant, Christina." She gave her a hug, and Antonio saw his wife whisper something to her in private.

"It's already being taken care of," Lindsay whispered back, but Antonio read her lips.

Intrigued, he couldn't wait to get his bride alone, but no one was ready to leave the reception yet and Zach had snatched her away to dance. He decided now was the time to dance with his mother, then his mother-in-law.

The queen gave him a hug before he danced her around the terrace. "You're going to have to keep an eye on that one," she said, eyeing Christina, who was still whirling around with Zach. "She isn't quite as docile as I remember."

"She's her own person," Antonio replied with the sudden thrilling realization that his new bride might mean more to him than he could have imagined.

"Indeed she is. You both look perfectly marvelous together. She's changed so much since the engagement that I hardly recognize her. You have no idea how glad I am that you've come home for good to settle down. A man needs marriage, and your marriage is good for the monarchy. I'm very happy with you today."

"Thank you, Mama." Except that marriage hadn't stopped his parents from having their offstage affairs.

He twirled her back to the table and asked Christina's mother to dance. She had been a former fashion model and was still a very attractive woman. But as he gazed at Christina, who was laughing quietly with Zach, he thought she was the *real* beauty. Not only in her appearance, but in her character.

"Are you sorry our daughter wanted the wedding here instead of at the cathedral in Voti?"

"Anything but. Don't you think every woman should be able to have the wedding of her dreams where she wants it?"

"But you're the crown prince."

Antonio smiled at her. "Tonight I'm a new bridegroom and I can't imagine a more perfect setting for Christina and me than this delightful spot in Tuscany."

"Then I'm glad for both of you. You make a stunning pair."

"Grazie."

He could still hear Christina's words when she'd told him what it was like at boarding school. *We were all a bunch of girls who'd rather be home. We all had a case of homesickness and waited for the letters that didn't arrive.* The emptiness in her voice had conveyed pain, even after all these years.

If he didn't do anything else, he would make certain she didn't feel pain because of him. "Did you visit her in Africa?"

"We made it over once and were guests in the palace of Marusha's parents. They're very westernized there."

"Your daughter has made a big contribution. It's no small thing she has done to help those in poverty."

"I'm very proud of her."

He was glad to hear it. On that note he danced her back to the table. After thanking her, he went over to the table where Marusha was seated and asked her to dance with him. The charming woman had come with her husband. He gave her a turn around the terrace.

"You honor me, Your Highness. I'm very happy Christina is your bride. We hope you'll both come to Kenya and stay with us."

"I've always wanted to travel there and promise to visit you when the time is right. You honor us by coming. Christina thinks the world of you and your family."

"We feel the same. Thank you."

Once she was seated, Antonio hurried to find Christina, who was talking to Elena. His sister smiled at him. "It's about time you paid attention to your bride."

"First I want a dance with you, little sister, if it's all right with my wife."

Christina darted him a serious glance. "She's the reason we even know each other. You're welcome to enjoy her for as long as you want."

He knew she meant that and moved Elena around the terrace. She had a gleam in her eye. "Having fun, brother dear? More than you thought?"

"Much more," he confessed.

"Christina has that effect on people. Mother can't get over the change in her. I told her that Christina is like the woman in the stone. All Michelangelo had to do was chip away at the marble until her beauty emerged for all to see."

His sister had just put the right words to his thoughts. "It's a perfect analogy."

She studied his features. "It's growing dark. Are you ready to leave the party?" she asked with a sly smile.

"The truth?"

"Always."

"I feel like I did the first time I had to jump out of a plane during my military service."

Elena chuckled. "Since you survived, I'm not worried."

"In all honesty, I haven't made this easy for Christina by maintaining distance between us over the last four years."

"Don't worry about it. She married you today and I think you've both met your match. I'm so happy for both of you I could burst. Don't let me keep you from whisking your bride away." She kissed his cheek and hurried off.

He was left standing there while her last comment sank in. Antonio hated to admit he felt nervous for what was to come. He'd be taking his wife upstairs to the bridal chamber. This was a new experience for him. Taking a fortifying breath, he made a beeline for Christina, who was talking to more guests.

Lindsay came up to him. "Christina still needs to throw her bridal bouquet to the crowd. If you're ready, take her to the front of the palazzo and I'll make the announcement to the guests to follow you."

"Thank you for all you've done."

"It has been my pleasure."

He kissed her cheek before reaching for

his wife. Christina's gaze flicked to his. "What is it?"

"We have one more ritual to perform." He picked up the bridal bouquet. After putting it in her hands, he slid an arm around her slender waist. Her lovely body was a perfect fit for him.

"I already know where I'm going to throw it," she whispered as they left the terrace and walked around to the front entrance of the palazzo.

"So do I," he drawled.

"Antonio?" She eyed him with surprising tenderness. "Thank you for dancing with Marusha. To dance with the future king had to be one of the big highlights of her life."

"I wanted a chance to thank her for coming. She's been your true friend all these years. I have a feeling you two are going to miss each other."

"That's something I want to talk to you about, but we'll discuss it later."

An alarm bell went off in Antonio's head. Did Christina want to go back to Africa? She'd lived a whole period of her life there that he knew nothing about. In fairness, she didn't know details about his former life either. While he stood there filled with new questions that needed answers, the guests had congregated in the courtyard.

Before he knew what she was doing, his wife cleared her throat and faced the crowd. "Antonio and I want to thank you all for coming to share in our beautiful wedding day. I'm one of the lucky girls in the world who actually got to marry a real prince. His kindness to his sister, Princess Elena, my dearest friend, proved his princely worth to me years ago. I can honestly say there's not another man like him, prince or otherwise. So this is for you, Elena. May you find your own wonderful prince too!"

Christina turned her back to the crowd and threw the bouquet in a southeasterly direction that was no mistake with Elena standing there. It was no accident that everyone made room around his sister so she could catch it. Then a roar of approval and clapping burst from the crowd. Antonio's breath caught. With that speech she'd ensured her place in everyone's heart as their queen-to-be.

Filled with emotion, he put his arm around her shoulders and pressed a kiss to her lips.

She kissed him back and it felt convincing, but was this a show for the camera? He'd felt a distinct spark when they kissed at the altar. But if it had only been on his part, he didn't want to believe it right now. Was she nervous too?

Without asking her permission, he grasped her hand and drew her along with him to the inside of the palazzo. He leaned back against the closed door, still holding her hand. Now that the moment was here to be alone with her, he felt slightly breathless. The wedding night was upon them.

"Are you up to climbing to the third floor?"

The bridal suite.

Their bridal suite now. The kiss Antonio had given her in front of the palazzo felt… hungry. In that moment she'd experienced an answering rush of desire that took her by storm. Her fantasy had taken on a new dimension. What was going on with her?

"I think I can about make it," she teased, and started her ascent. But after a few steps she picked up her gown to give her the freedom to hurry the rest of the way. His footsteps followed, keeping pace with the thundering of her heart.

She almost ran down the hallway to the bridal suite. Before she reached the doors, he caught up to her and picked her up in his arms. "Oh—" she half squealed, surprised her gown didn't hinder him. She knew her husband was strong, but being held close to him like this made her realize what a rock-hard physique he possessed, and he smelled wonderful.

Their faces were only inches apart. He smiled into her eyes. The blue of his irises had a depth of brilliance that ignited every pulse point in her body. "I don't know about you, but I've been looking forward to this all day." He slowly lowered his mouth to hers and began kissing her.

A burst of desire swept through her. Things were moving much faster than she'd anticipated and she found herself kissing him back with an urgency she couldn't seem to suppress. What was happening was perfectly natural for a grown man and woman on their wedding night, but they had come to this marriage as friends from a long time ago. He'd never held her, or danced with her or kissed her, in Switzerland.

When she could take a breath she said, "If you keep this up, our dinner will get cold."

"What dinner?" His gaze was focused on her mouth.

"The one we didn't eat. It's waiting for us out on the terrace of our suite."

"Was that what you were whispering to Lindsay about?"

She nodded.

"I must say I'd much prefer eating with you alone up here. I like the way my wife thinks."

Christina was glad he felt that way, because she needed time to get used to him. A meal would give both of them a chance to unwind while they anticipated their wedding night. Now that the moment was here, she didn't know what to do and felt so awkward she hoped he couldn't sense it.

Antonio gave her another swift kiss on the lips and managed to open the door. He walked through the foyer of the semidark suite and made it as far as the bedchamber before putting her down. She eased away far enough to remove the veil and tiara.

He knew she needed some privacy before they did anything else. "I'll be back in a few minutes." He pressed a kiss to her lips. "Don't start dinner without me."

"I won't. Your bags should be in the sitting room."

"I'll find them."

Much as he was reluctant to let her go, he needed to make her more comfortable. After giving her upper arms a quick squeeze, he left the bridal chamber for the other part of the suite. Spotting his bags, he went into the bathroom down the hall to freshen up. It was a relief to discard his sash and ceremonial dress jacket. This was a brand-new experience for both of them. Tonight he wanted to do everything right for her.

Hoping he'd given her enough time, he left the bathroom and started back to the bridal suite. He'd undone his shirt at the neck and rolled his sleeves up to the elbows.

Against the darkened sky, the candles flickering from the terrace table bathed Christina in soft light. As she leaned over in her exquisite wedding dress to pour their wine, he noticed the glory of her midlength hair where the strands of gold gleamed among the red. It looked so thick and sleek he longed to run his hands through it.

She must have sensed his presence and gave him a sideward glance. Again the candles flickered, turning her eyes to a shimmery silver. His bride had come to this earth with her own unique color scheme, one that resonated with him in ways he hadn't noticed at the age of eighteen. His fifteen-year-old sister and her friend had been too young for him to appreciate the sight he was being treated to tonight.

Between her classic features with those high cheekbones and passionate red mouth, the blood was pounding in his veins. His gaze fell lower to the feminine outline of her body in her gown. While they'd danced, she filled his arms in all the right places and was the perfect height for him.

Her choice of wedding gown had pleased him immensely. She looked demure, but her coloring added the dash of sensuality he'd noticed the first moment he saw her in the chapel.

Christina might not have been aware of

it, but he'd watched the males in the crowd admiring her all evening long.

For the first time he wondered how many men she'd known who'd more than admired her. Though it was a little late to question what her love life had been like prior to the actual preparations for their wedding, he couldn't help but wonder. He felt as if he were swimming in waters over his head.

Her eyes played over him as he moved toward her. He liked the way she was looking at him. When she reached for her wineglass, he picked up his. "This wine comes from the Brunello grapes grown in this vineyard."

Antonio swirled it around in his glass. "That's very fitting. I'm sure it will be delicious. A toast to my wife, who has already made my life infinitely richer by simply agreeing to marry me. *Salud!*" He touched his glass to hers before they both drank some.

She unexpectedly raised her glass again and touched his. "To my husband. You never let your sister down or betrayed her trust. Because of that you've won mine. To you, Antonio. *Salud!* You'll make the finest king our country has ever known."

"If that happens, it's because you're at my side." His throat swelled with emotion, making it difficult to swallow his second taste of the fruity wine.

"Shall we sit down to eat? I'm sure you're as ravenous as I am." She seated herself before he could help her.

They both tucked in to the heavenly food. She ate with an appetite. He liked that. Most women of his acquaintance ate rabbit food—whether to impress him or not—but not Christina. There was nothing fake about her. *That* was what impressed him.

When she lifted her eyes to him he said, "The little speech you gave in front of the palazzo blew me away."

"It did?"

"How could it not? I thought no other man could be luckier than I am to have you for my wife."

"I feel the same way about you."

"Christina—I know I've put you in an impossible situation."

"You don't have to say anything, Antonio. I understand. That's behind us now."

"No, it isn't. Not until I tell you why."

She had hold of her wineglass stem, but

she didn't lift it to her lips while she waited for his explanation. Looking at her right now, he didn't think he'd ever seen so beautiful a woman.

"In a word, I was afraid."

Her delicate eyebrows frowned. "Of what?"

"That once I was in Africa where we could really be alone, you might tell me the engagement was off and send me packing."

She sounded aghast and let go of the glass to put a hand to her throat. "I would never have done that to you."

"Then you're a woman in a million. Who else would have sacrificed her personal happiness for the greater good of someone, something else?"

"Our circumstances were very unusual, but I *am* happy."

He shook his head. "You don't need to pretend with me. This is truth time. I did something terribly selfish to ask you to marry me."

A pained look entered her eyes. "Is this your way of telling me you wish we hadn't gone through with the wedding?"

"No, Christina, no—" He reached across the table and grasped both her hands. "I'm just thankful you consented to be my bride. If you'll let me, I'd like us to start over again. Through Elena we've been friends for years, but you and I don't know each other. I want to get to know all about you. What are the things you love to do? What are the things you hope to do?"

Her silvery gaze enveloped him. "Besides grow old with you?"

"Yes. I'd like to learn it all."

"I'm a pretty normal woman, Antonio. I like reading books and eating chocolate. I like spending time with my friends, especially your sister. I love Africa and the time I spent there helping others. But I suppose my greatest wish would be to have a family of my own. When I first visited the Kikuyu villages with all the adorable children, I hungered for a child of my own. How do you feel about children?"

"I want them too, Christina."

"But I want to take care of them myself. Even if I'll be queen, I want to be their mother in the truest sense of the word."

"So you don't want to send them away to boarding school?"

"Why? It doesn't make sense to me that

if you have a child, you would send it away as soon as possible."

He released her hands. "You're talking about yourself."

"Yes."

He saw her eyes glaze over.

"I wanted my mother and father during my growing-up years. If you and I have a baby, would you want it to leave us before it was time to let him or her go? Did you like being sent away to boarding school?"

"I didn't have a choice."

"But did you like it?"

"No. I've never admitted that out loud."

"Neither did Elena."

"I know."

"But *we'll* be the parents," Christina said, then added in an anxious tone, "Will our son have a choice? You say you want to know all about me. If you tell me our children will have to leave home before I'm ready to see them go, I couldn't bear it. Why have them at all?"

Antonio got out of the chair and went around to hunker down beside her. He grasped the hand closest to him. "Look at me." She finally did his bidding. "I was wrong not to come to Africa. We did need time to talk about all these things so I could reassure you."

He heard her heavy sigh before she spoke. "I'm sorry I've turned this beautiful night into something else. Forgive me."

"There's nothing to forgive. You have my word that we'll keep any children we have with us for as long as they want to be with us. The only time they'll have a nanny is if you need to attend a royal function with me."

Her eyes lit up again. "Honest? Is that a promise?"

He could deny her nothing. "I swear it."

"Oh, Antonio. You've made me so happy."

To crush her in his arms was all he had on his mind, but he wanted to give her time and feel comfortable with him. "I was afraid you were going to tell me that you wanted to live in Africa part of the year."

"My life is with you, but I'd love it if we took some trips there together one day. Maybe when our children are old enough to enjoy the animal life? But we've been talking about me. What is one of your dreams?"

"I'm a pretty normal man too. I want a family. I want to be a success at what I do. Because I'll be king, I want to change the country's impression of a monarchy that has shown a breakdown in the old values."

"Like what for instance?"

"The excess spending for one. There are so many areas that need change. But I'm boring you."

"Never."

"Spoken like my queen already." He got to his feet and drew her over to the terrace railing with him. He looked out over the peaceful Tuscan landscape. His pulse throbbed with new life. He wasn't the same man who'd slipped the brooch into the bedchamber earlier in the day.

If he had to describe his feelings at this minute, he was excited for what was to come. When he'd anticipated his wedding weeks ago, he didn't count on being thrilled by this woman who surprised him at every turn. He no longer felt trapped.

Things were going so well he didn't dare make the wrong move until she was ready for the physical side of their marriage. For them to get through the wedding without problems when they were virtual strangers led him to believe they could turn their marriage into something strong, maybe even wonderful given enough time.

He already felt strong feelings for her, which surprised him. They'd discussed one crucial element concerning their marriage by talking about the children they would have. But as near to each other as they were physically right now, they were still worlds apart.

"Christina?" He turned to her and cupped her face in his hands. "Tonight I'm happier than any man has a right to be." He lowered his head and closed his mouth over hers. The taste and feel of her set his pulse racing. "You're the most wonderful thing to come into my life."

Antonio pressed kisses over every feature. "I need to get closer to you. Would you like me to undo the buttons at the back of your wedding dress before I change?"

He saw a little nerve jump at the base of her throat. His bride was nervous. That was his fault for not visiting her and letting her get comfortable with him.

"Yes, please."

She turned, reminding him of a modest young maiden. It brought out his tenderest feelings as he began undoing them from the top of her neckline to the bottom, which ran below her waistline. His fingers brushed her warm skin as he set about freeing her trembling body. Never had he enjoyed a task more.

"A-are you finished?" she stammered.

He smiled to himself. "Not quite." When he was done, he lifted her hair and kissed the nape of her neck. Her mane felt like silk. "There. You're free," he whispered, and turned her around. The sleeves and bodice of her gown were loose. All he had to do...

But he didn't dare. "I don't think you have any idea how lovely you are. I want to kiss you, *esposa mia*. Really kiss you." He found her trembling mouth and began to devour her. The few kisses they'd shared up to now bore little resemblance to the desire he felt for her as she responded with growing hunger.

He clasped her against him, feeling her heart thundering into his. Antonio had an almost primitive need to make love to her, but not this stand-up kind of loving. He wanted her in his bed and was so enthralled by her he moaned when she unexpectedly tore her lips from his and eased away from him.

"Christina?" He had to catch his breath. "Have I frightened you?"

"No." She shook her head, clutching her gown to her.

He could tell she was as shocked as he was by what had just happened. He needed to reassure her. "This has been a huge day, especially for you. I'm going to let you go right now. Since we have to be up early to leave on our honeymoon, I'll bid you *buonanotte, bellissima*, and make myself a bed on the couch in the sitting room."

CHAPTER FOUR

CHRISTINA STARED AFTER her new husband, so startled by his sudden departure she could weep. She'd been on fire for him and had been ready to go wherever he led. But in the moment that she'd tried to catch a breath, Antonio left her in a dissatisfied condition.

Was it possible a groom could have nerves like the bride? Confused over what had happened, she blew out the candles and walked to the bedroom. After stepping out of her wedding dress, she laid it over a chair with the veil on top. She put her satin slippers on the floor and placed the tiara on the dresser. They were remnants of the happiest day of her life.

She slipped on a nightgown before brushing her teeth. Then she turned out the lights and got into bed. How could she possibly sleep when her body was throbbing with needs she'd never felt before? He'd awakened a fire in her, but she hadn't known how to handle it when he told her he'd make a bed on the couch for the night. She hadn't had the temerity to go after him.

Sleep must have come, but she awakened early and finished her packing. Making use of the time until Antonio joined her, she'd touched up her pedicure and manicure. Her nails were done in a two-toned nude shade that matched everything and did justice to her royal antique-gold wedding band and diamond ring.

Since they'd be flying to Paris and would be the target of the paparazzi, Christina had chosen to wear an elegant-looking white two-piece suit from her new royal trousseau. The jacket with sleeves to the elbow fit at the waist. The high neck was half collared and there were pockets on the jacket as well as the skirt. She wore the brooch above the left pocket.

It was the perfect lightweight summery outfit to wear while walking around the City of Lights. Low-heeled off-white pumps and an off-white jacquard designed clutch bag with gloves completed her ensemble.

She'd worn her hair parted sideways into a high bun with one loose, hanging side longer than the other. Two white sticks for her hair with pearl tips matched her pearl stud earrings. Christina hadn't worn perfume in Africa in order to avoid attracting insects. Back home now, she used a soap with a delicious flowery scent. Her makeup consisted of a tarte lip tint. She needed no other color.

When she was ready, she walked to the door of the sitting room and knocked. "Antonio? Our breakfast is waiting."

"*Grazie.* I'll be right out." His deep-timbred male voice curled through her. It sounded an octave lower than usual. He must have barely awakened.

She wandered out to the terrace to wait for him. Her eyes filled with the beauty of the Tuscan countryside. The peaceful scene reminded her of a picture in a storybook where the rows of the vineyard formed perfect lines. All around it the gold and green of the landscape undulated off in the distance dotted with a farmhouse here and a red-roofed villa there.

Too bad she felt anything but peaceful inside.

All of a sudden she sensed she wasn't alone and turned to discover a clean-shaven Antonio studying her from the doorway wearing a casual summer suit in a tan color with a cream sport shirt unbuttoned at the throat. With his olive skin and rugged features, he was so gorgeous she couldn't believe she was married to him.

"Buongiorno, esposo mio," she said softly.

His blue gaze roved over her body from her hair to her heels, missing nothing in between. She'd never felt him look at her that way before, as if she were truly desirable. Her legs went weak because she hadn't expected that look after he decided not to sleep with her last night. She honestly didn't know what to expect.

"How are you this morning?" he asked in a husky tone of voice. A small nerve throbbed at the corner of his mouth. What were his emotions after having gone to his own bed last night instead of spending it in hers?

"I'm fine, thank you. I'm excited that we'll

be walking along the Champs-Élysées later on today. Aren't you?"

A strange smile broke the line of his mouth. "Shall we eat while we talk over our itinerary?" A question instead of an answer. Something was wrong.

He held out a chair for her. When she sat down, his hands molded to her shoulders for a moment. Warmth from his fingers coiled through her body. "As bewitching as you were to this man's eyes last night, I find the sight of you right now even more beguiling."

Because of the way he'd been looking at her when no one else was around, she believed he'd meant what he just said. But she hadn't been beguiling enough to go to bed with her. She decided to accept the compliment graciously instead of throwing it back in his face.

"Thank you."

"You're welcome." His hands left her shoulders and he took his place across the table from her. They both started eating the rolls and fruit. After drinking some coffee he said, "How did you sleep?"

"The truth?"

"Always."

"Probably as poorly as you. I doubt that couch was long enough to accommodate your feet." She was glad to hear a chuckle come from him. His eyes lit up with amusement. "When everyone sees us, they'll think we're sleep-deprived because of a passion-filled wedding night and they'll be happy to think that a new royal heir could be on the way already. You know that's what's on everyone's mind."

He flashed her a piercing glance through narrowed lids. "But our business is our own."

"Of course."

After eating another roll, he sat back in the chair. "My mother left it to my father to give me some last-minute advice."

That didn't surprise Christina. "What did he have to say?"

"It isn't what they said. It's what they did."

"I'm not following you."

"Read this." He handed her a note from his suit jacket pocket.

She opened it.

Dear Antonio, your mother and I want you to have the perfect honeymoon. We know you wanted to spend a few days touring Paris and the environs before the coronation next week. But we've thought of something much better and it has all been arranged. All you have to do is be ready by eight in the morning. A helicopter will fly you to Genoa, where you'll take the royal jet to a dream spot for your vacation. It's a place neither you nor Christina has been to before. As always we remain your devoted parents.

They weren't going to Paris?

Her pulse raced. She'd thought there would be so much to do there and they'd have time to get to know each other while seeing the sights. Just what kind of dream vacation did his parents have in mind?

To be gone for a whole week together alone— It worried her that in a week's time he might find out she was unlovable. That old fear never quite went away.

What was Antonio's reaction to the news? Christina's first impulse was to tell him she didn't want to go on any dream vacation. But she couldn't refuse to do the first thing he was asking of her, especially when it was a wedding present from the king and queen themselves.

"I can hear every thought running through your head, Christina. The look in your eyes is all I need to see to know this is the last thing you expected or wanted. If it's any help, it's a surprise to me too. The idea of our honeymoon being scripted by my parents at the taxpayers' expense is typical of the lavish way they've lived their lives and expected me to do the same. If you still want to go to Paris, that's what we'll do."

"And hurt your parents?" It took a courageous man to say that to her. She was touched that he would put her feelings first. Her watch said it was almost eight now. "No, Antonio. We have the rest of our lives to plan our own vacations when we can get away. I don't want us to start off our marriage by alienating your parents. What difference does it make where we go?"

Something flickered in the recesses of his eyes. "Thank you for saying that. I like it that my new bride is adaptable and sensitive enough not to hurt their feelings. Have you done all your packing?"

"Yes." It was a good thing Elena had done

some shopping with her and had insisted on her buying a couple of bikinis. "You never know when you need beachwear," her friend had confided. Maybe Elena had known about the location of the vacation spot her parents had planned for them and wanted Christina prepared for any eventuality. "How about you, Antonio?"

"I'm ready as I ever will be."

"Then I'll freshen up and meet you down-stairs." She got up from the table and hurried into the bathroom for one last look in the mirror. After applying a new coat of lipstick, she walked into the bedroom and noticed her suitcase was missing. She could count on Lindsay and Louisa to make certain her wedding things were packed and returned to the royal palace in Voti.

All she needed was her purse and gloves. When she left the bridal suite and started down the stairs, she discovered Antonio waiting for her in the foyer of the palazzo.

He stood there looking tall and heart-breakingly handsome. His brilliant blue gaze swept over her in a way that sent her pulse racing. "Will you accuse me of using a platitude to tell you how beautiful you look this morning?"

"Even with bags under my eyes from lack of sleep?" But she smiled as she said it.

"Even then," he murmured. A tiny smile lifted one corner of his lips. "As you said earlier, any onlookers will speculate on the reason why and consider me the luckiest of men."

She took the last step, bringing her closer. "You're good, Antonio. I'll give you that."

He cocked his head. "What do you mean?"

"I think you know. Aren't you afraid all these compliments are going to turn my head?"

The smile disappeared. "If you want to know the truth, I'm afraid they won't."

While she stood there confused again and wondering how much truth was behind his statement, Guido, his father's chief of staff, opened the doors. "Your Highness? Princess Christina?"

Guido had addressed her as *Princess*. She'd better get used to the title, but the appellation was still foreign to her.

"If you're both ready, your cases are stowed in the limousine. Your helicopter is waiting in Monte Calanetti to fly you to Genoa."

"*Grazie*, Guido. We're coming."

She preceded Antonio out to the smoked-glass black limousine with the royal crest on the hood ornament. Guido held the rear door open for her so she could climb in, then shut the door. Antonio went around the other side and got in, shutting the door behind him. He slid close to her while they both attached their seat belts.

"This is nice," he murmured, and grasped her hand. "I'm excited to be going off on a trip with my new wife. I only wish I knew where."

She glanced at him out of the corner of her eye. "Your sister may have given me a hint, but I didn't realize it at the time."

"What did she say?"

"She made sure I bought some bathing suits when we went shopping. Did you pack one?"

"I'm sure mine is in my case somewhere."

"Do you think Hawaii or the Caribbean? I've never been to either destination."

"I have." He released her hand long enough to pull the note from his pocket. "According to this, it's someplace where neither of us has been before."

"That's right. I forgot."

"Our parents probably collaborated. It ought to be interesting."

"I agree. From what Elena has told me, you've been all over the world."

He smiled. "Let's put it this way. I've traveled over many countries without ever landing."

Christina returned his smile. She'd taken many helicopter trips with Marusha into the more inaccessible areas of Kenya's forested interior, so she was no stranger to the sensation of liftoff or landing. Before she knew it, they'd arrived on the outskirts of the village where their helicopter was waiting.

Antonio helped her out of the limo into one of the rear seats of the helicopter. He climbed in next to her while Guido placed their cases inside, then got in the copilot's seat for the short flight to Genoa. Passing over the Tuscan countryside was a constant delight.

Once they boarded the royal jet with its insignia in huge gold lettering, Christina was introduced to the pilot and copilot before being given a tour. She was struck by the staggering opulence inside and out. To her mind, the platinum curving couches, mirrored ceilings and ornate bathroom were out-of-this-world outrageous.

With an office, a gourmet kitchen and two bedrooms, all extravagant to the point of being ridiculous, she imagined the plane that contained a cockpit meant for the emperor of the universe must have cost in the region of millions upon millions of dollars.

Antonio must have been watching her, because he said in a quiet voice, "Is there any question in your mind why our country is outraged by the unnecessary spending of my own parents? Papa bought this off an oil-rich sheik. When I'm king, I have every intention of selling it to the highest bidder and using the money to bolster Halencia's economy and put more funds in your charity foundation."

When she thought of the relief that money could bring to the Kikuyu people, she wanted to throw her arms around his neck in joy, but she didn't dare with Guido and the steward in hearing distance.

After they sat down on one of the couches,

Guido made a surprising announcement. "This is where I leave you, Your Highnesses. When you reach your destination, you'll be met and taken to your vacation paradise. After the plane lands, you'll be flown in a helicopter to your own private paradise. There'll be no phone, television or internet service there."

What?

While she sat there stunned, she could tell by the lines around his mouth that Antonio wasn't amused either. "Guido? You've gotten us this far, but I refuse to travel any farther until you tell me where we're going."

"I suppose it couldn't hurt to say that you'll be arriving on the other side of the world in approximately twenty-one hours from now."

"That's not much help," Antonio said in a clipped voice.

"I'm only following the king's orders. Is there anything I can do for you before I leave?"

Antonio turned to her. "How about you, Christina?"

She had compassion for Guido, who was

loyal to his king first. "I don't need anything. Thank you for everything you've done."

"You're welcome. Enjoy your honeymoon." He bowed to Antonio before leaving the plane.

In a few minutes the engines screamed to life and the fasten-seat-belts sign flashed on. Before long the jet headed into the sun. Once they'd achieved cruising speed, they got up from the couch and moved to sit in the lavish dining area where the steward served them a fabulous lunch.

"Don't be upset with Guido. It's obvious your parents' big surprise is important to him and to them."

One eyebrow lifted. "Twenty-one hours one way takes a lot of fuel. Round-trip means thousands more dollars being paid out from the public coffers. It isn't right."

She sat back while she sipped her coffee. "I agree, and I admire your desire to change the dynamics of the L'Accardi family's spending habits. But for now, why don't we decide to be Jack and Jill, two normal people who got married on a whim, and have just been given a windfall from their oil-rich uncle in Texas who wants to make us happy."

"Oil?"

"Why not? When we return to civilization, that's the time to start trimming the budget."

When she didn't think it was possible, he chuckled. "Jack and Jill, eh?"

She nodded. "One of the American girls from Texas at the boarding school had the name Jill, and her brother's name was Jack."

By now his eyes were smiling. "I'll go along with that idea. What do you say we go to one of the bedrooms and watch a movie where we can be comfortable?"

Each bedroom had a built-in theater. She wiped her mouth with a napkin. "I'll find my suitcase and change my clothes."

He reached across the table and grasped her hand. "I'm sorry you're not able to show off that lovely white outfit in Paris."

A warm smile broke out on her face. "Don't be." She wouldn't forget the way he'd stared at her when he walked out on the terrace earlier that morning. Christina had seen a glint of genuine male appreciation in his eyes that brought her great pleasure. "We'll do Paris one of these days."

Feeling his gaze on her retreating back, she walked through the compartment and found the bedroom where both their cases had been placed. She took hers and crossed the hall into the other bedroom.

After putting it on the queen-size bed, she found a pair of lightweight pants in dusky blue and a filmy long-sleeved shirt with a floral pattern of light and dark blues combined with pink. It draped beautifully against her body to the hips.

The white suit went in the closet before she slipped into her casual clothes and put on bone-colored leather sandals. After removing the pearl tipped sticks from her hair, she exchanged the pearl studs for gold earrings mounted with star-shaped blue sapphire stones. As she was applying a fresh coat of lipstick, she heard a knock on the door.

"Antonio?"

He opened it but didn't enter. "Come on over to the other bedroom when you're ready."

Her heart started to thud. "I'll be there in a minute."

Antonio had changed into jeans and a sport shirt. Normally he would have put on the bottoms of a pair of sweats and nothing else for the twenty-one-hour flight. But out of consideration for Christina, he needed to make his way carefully for this journey into the unknown. Their honeymoon was in the process of becoming a fait accompli.

He'd experienced two heart attacks already: one at the altar when his fiancée appeared in her white wedding dress and lace veil. The other attack happened this morning when he first saw her on the terrace ready for their trip to Paris wearing a stunning white outfit. When he heard her call out his name just now, he should have known to brace himself for the third attack.

"Enter if you dare," he teased. Antonio had stretched out on the bed with his head and back propped against the headboard using a pillow for a buffer.

"Ready or not," she countered, and came into the room. The incredibly beautiful woman dressed in blue appeared, and the sight almost caused him to drop the remote. With her shiny hair, she lit up any room she entered. How could he have ignored her for so long? The few phone calls and visits to her had been made out of duty. The busy life he'd been leading in California had included hard work *and* one certain woman when he had the time.

Thoughts of his future marriage for the good of the country had only played on the edge of his consciousness, as did the woman who'd been thousands of miles away in Kenya. He couldn't go back and fix things, but he could shower her with attention now. They didn't know each other well yet, but had made a start last night when their passion ignited.

Antonio recognized that he needed to treat her the way he would any beautiful woman he'd just met and wanted to get to know much better. He patted her side of the bed. "Come and join me. We have a choice of five films without my having to move from this spot."

She laughed and pulled a pillow out from under the quilt. The next thing he knew she'd thrown it at the foot of the bed and lain down on her stomach so she could watch the screen located on the other side of the bedroom. "Why don't you start the one you'd like to see without telling me what it is?" she said over her shoulder.

Christina made an amazing sight with

those long legs lying enticingly close to him. "What if you don't like it?"

"I like all kinds of movies and will watch it because I want to know what makes my husband tick."

His heart skipped a beat. "You took the words out of my mouth." He clicked to the disk featuring a Neapolitan Mafia gangster film. "I only saw part of this when it first came out."

"I'm sure I haven't seen it. Italian films are hard to come by when you're out in the bush. This is fun!"

He found it more than fun to be watching it with the woman he'd just married. She made the usual moans and groans throughout. When it concluded she turned on her side and propped her head to look back at him. "I heard that the Camorra Mafia from Naples was the inspiration for that film. Were there really a hundred gangs, do you think?"

"I do."

"Did any cross the water into our country?"

"Three families that we know of."

"Do they still exist?"

"Yes, but were given Halencian citizenship at a time when our borders were more porous. They're no longer a problem. What I'm concerned about is creating high-tech jobs. Tourism and agriculture alone aren't going to sustain our growing population. I have many plans and have been laying the groundwork to establish software companies and a robotics plant, all of which can operate here to build Halencian industry."

"So *that's* what you've been doing in San Francisco all these years. No wonder you didn't come home often."

"Are you accusing me of being a workaholic?"

Her eyelids narrowed. "Are you?"

"I make time to play."

"Since I won't be able to go to sleep for a long time, what can I do for you, my husband?"

"How about reading to me?"

The question pleased her no end. "You'd like that?"

"I saw a book in your suitcase. Have you read it already?"

"I'm in the middle of it."

"What's it called?"

"*Cry, the Beloved Country* by Alan Paton. He wrote about South Africa and the breakdown of the tribal system. It's not the part of Africa I know, but it's so wonderful I'm compelled to finish the book."

"I never got around to reading it," he said.

"Tell you what. I'll read you the blurb on the flyleaf. If it interests you, I'll read from the beginning until you fall asleep."

"I'm surprised you don't carry a Kindle with you. Aren't physical books heavy to carry when traveling?"

"They can be, but I really like to hold a book in my hands. They're like an old friend I can see peeking at me from the bookshelf, teasing me to come and read again."

"I've decided you're a Renaissance woman, Christina."

"That's a curious word."

"It really describes you. You're a very intelligent woman. I see in you a revival of vigor and an interest in life that escapes most people. You're more intriguing than you know."

If she was intriguing, that was something. "When did you discover that?" she asked without looking at him.

"It happened when you were just fifteen. I drove you and Elena to an old monastery in the woods above Lake Geneva. When we went inside, you were able to translate all the Latin inscriptions in those glass cases. I detested Latin and at eighteen I still needed a tutor for it. To hear you translating for us, I was so stunned at your expertise, it left me close to speechless. Do you remember that time?"

He remembered that? It caused her pulse to pick up speed. "Yes. I was showing off to you so you wouldn't think that your sister was spending time with a complete numbskull. My mother hated it that I was such a bookworm and would rather read than go to tea with a bunch of girls who only talked about boys and clothes."

"This conversation is getting interesting. When *did* you first become interested in boys?"

"Actually I was crazy about them at a very early age." Pictures of Prince Antonio and Princess Elena were constantly in the news. From the time she was about eight, she always liked to see photos of the famous brother and sister in the newspaper accompanying their family on a ski trip or some such thing.

He was the country's darling. By the time she met him in person, she'd already developed a crush on him that only grew after being with him. Of course all the silliness ended when she left Montreux and had new experiences in Africa. Once in a while she and Marusha would see him in the news, but until Elena's brush with the law he'd been as distant to her as another galaxy.

Antonio broke into laughter. "The secret life of Christina Rose. How scandalous."

She chuckled. "Marusha had plenty to tell me about tribal mating rituals of the Kikuyu. In fact, she kept me and Elena royally entertained most nights after lights went out. We'd stay up half the night talking. She had a crush on this security guard who was guarding a VIP at the Montreux Palace Hotel.

"You know how beautiful Marusha is. Well, we'd walk past him and she'd say things to him to capture his interest. He never spoke, but his eyes always watched her. He was tall, maybe six foot five, and he kept his arms folded. He was the most impressive figure I ever saw and I think he was the reason she could handle being in Montreux when she'd rather be home in Africa."

Laughter continued to rumble out of Antonio.

"Your sister had other interests. There was a drummer in the band that played at this one disco we were ordered not to visit. He was crazy about her and kept making dates with her. She only kept one of them. It was through him she met other guys, the kind she finally ended up with who got thrown in jail for drugs."

"Let's be thankful she has grown up now, but don't stop talking," Antonio murmured. "I could listen to you all night. What masculine interest did *you* have?"

Christina didn't dare tell him that there was no male to match Antonio. His image was the one she'd always carried in the back of her mind. "Oh… I always loved men in the old Italian movies. You know, Franco Nero, Marcello Mastroianni, Vittorio De Sica."

"No Halencian actors?"

"No. I've liked a couple of British actors too. Rufus Sewell…*ooh-la-la*." She grinned.

"Now, there is a male to die for! So, which actress did it for you?"

"That would be difficult to answer."

"You don't play fair. You manage to get a lot of information out of me, but I ask you one question and suddenly you play possum."

"What does that mean?"

"It means you play dead like a possum when you don't want to reveal yourself. The possum does it for protection. It's a very funny American expression and it describes you right now. What are you hiding from? Is the truth too scary for you?"

"Have a heart, Christina. I'm not nearly so terrible a womanizer as some of the tabloids have made me out to be. They're mostly lies."

"That's all right. You just keep telling yourself that. When I married you I forgave you for everything. But I've talked your ear off, so excuse me for a minute."

She hurried into the other bedroom and grabbed the book from the table, and then she returned to Antonio. "Are you still in the mood to be read to, or are you ready to confess your sins?"

"Yes and no."

He was hilarious.

"All right, then. Here's the quote from it. 'Cry, the beloved country, for the unborn child that is the inheritor of our fear.'" She read the rest.

A long silence ensued before Antonio murmured, "That's very moving. Tell me something honestly. Are you going to miss Africa too much?"

"What do you mean?"

"You've spent ten years of your life there. So many memories and friends you've made."

"Well, I'm hoping that from time to time I'll be able to fly to Nairobi to keep watch over the foundation, which I plan to continue with your permission."

"There's no question about that."

Good. "But our marriage is my first priority, and your needs come first and always will with me."

"You're wonderful, Christina, but that isn't what I asked, exactly. Did you leave your heart there?"

"Certainly a part of it, but I could ask you the same thing. Do you feel a strong tug when you think of San Francisco and the years you spent there?"

"I'd be a liar if I didn't say yes."

"I didn't expect you to say anything else. As for me, I've decided I have two homes. One there, where I've always been comfortable, and now the new one with you. I see them both being compatible. When you long for San Francisco and want to do business there, I'll understand."

"You'd love it there. I want to take you with me and show you around."

He couldn't have said anything to thrill her more. "And maybe you can fly to Africa with me for a little break from royal business."

"We'll make it happen."

She studied him for a long time. "Is there a woman you had to leave who's missing you right now? Maybe I should rephrase that. Is there someone you're missing horribly?"

Antonio should have seen these questions coming, particularly since he hadn't slept with her last night. "I haven't been a monk. What about you?"

A quick smile appeared. Her appeal was growing on him like mad. "I'm no nun."

For some odd reason he didn't like hearing that.

You hypocrite, Antonio. Did you want a bride as pure as the driven snow? Did you really expect her to give up men while she waited four years for you to decide when to claim her for your wife?

"Who was he?" His parents' affairs had jaded him.

"A doctor who'd come to Kenya to perform plastic surgery on some of the native children. Once I came back to Africa with the engagement ring on my finger, he left for England three days later."

"I kept you waiting four years," Antonio muttered in self-disgust.

A frown marred her features. "Antonio, none of that matters. I'm your wife! But you still haven't answered my question. Is there a woman who became of vital importance to you before you had to fly home to get married?"

He got off the bed. "The only woman of importance was one I got involved with before our engagement, Christina."

"Then you've known her a long time. If

there'd been no engagement, would you have married her?"

"That's hard to say. I might have if I'd decided to turn my back on my family and wanted to stay in California for the rest of my life. But when your call came telling me about Elena's problems and I talked to her, I realized how binding those family ties really are right from the cradle."

"I know that all too well," she whispered. Christina had obviously been talking about the relationship with her parents.

"The accident of my being born to a king and queen set me on a particular path. To marry a foreigner and deviate from it might bring me short-term pleasure. But I feared I'd end up living a lifetime of regret."

She shook her head. "How hard for both of you."

Her sincerity rang so true he felt it reach his bones. "Though I continued to see her after the engagement party, nothing was the same because we knew there would have to be an end. We soon said goodbye to each other.

"In a way it was a relief because to go on seeing her would not only have made a travesty of our engagement, but the situation was totally unfair to her and you. My sources at the palace confirmed that the country was suffering and there were plans afoot to abolish the monarchy. I knew it was only a matter of time before——"

"Before you had to come home and marry me to save the throne," she broke in. "I get it."

"Christina——" He approached her and grasped her hands. "Do you think it's possible for us to forget the past? You know what I mean. When I said my vows in the chapel, I meant what I said. I will love you and honor you all the days of my life. Can you still make that same commitment to me after knowing what I've told you?"

Her marvelous eyes filled with tears. "Oh, Antonio, I want you to know that when I made my vows at the altar, I was running on faith. Now that faith has been strengthened by what you've just admitted to me. If we have total honesty between us, then there's nothing to prevent us from trying to make this marriage work. You've always been the most handsome man I've ever known, so my attraction to you isn't a problem."

He kissed her fingers. "Can you forgive me for staying away from you before the wedding?"

"We've already had this discussion."

He slid his hands to her upper arms. "No woman but an angel like you would have sacrificed everything to enter into an engagement that didn't consider your own personal feelings in any way, shape or form. Forgive me, Christina. I don't like the man I was. I can only hope to become the man you're happy to be married to."

Her eyes roved over his features. "I liked the man you were. That man loved his sister enough to save her and their family from horrible embarrassment and scandal. She wasn't just any sister. She was the princess of Halencia, my friend. I loved you for loving her enough to help her.

"You have no idea what she did for me. She was the only person in my world besides my great-aunt Sofia who was good to me. Elena was the person I cried to every time I was hurt by my parents, especially my father, who wished I'd been born a boy." The tears trickled down her flushed cheeks.

Antonio sucked in his breath. "*Grazie a*

Dio, you're exactly who you are." He started kissing the tears away. When he reached her mouth he couldn't stop himself from covering it with his own. The taste of her excited him. Without her wedding dress on, he could draw her close and feel the contours of her beautiful body through the thin fabric of her shirt. Her fragrance worked like an aphrodisiac on his senses, which had come alive.

"Bellissima."

CHAPTER FIVE

THE FIRST TIME Christina had heard Antonio use the word *bellissima*, he'd said it in a teasing jest outside the door of the bridal suite. Just now he'd said it because she could sense his physical desire for her. After last night, there was no mistaking their attraction to each other. But she needed to use her head and not get swept away by passion until they'd spent more time together.

He'd wanted to put off making love to her last night. She was glad of it now. They did need more time to explore each other's minds first. Antonio might have walked away from the love of his life in San Francisco, but that didn't mean the memories didn't linger.

Christina could make love with him and pretend all was well, but she knew that until she held a place in his heart, then making love wouldn't have the same meaning for either of them. She wanted their first time to happen when it was right.

As soon as he lifted his mouth, she eased out of his arms. Avoiding his gaze she said, "I'm going to freshen up before dinner. Where do you want to eat?"

"How about the other bedroom? There'll be other films to pick from. Your choice. I'll tell the steward to bring it in ten minutes."

"Good. After our fabulous lunch, I can't believe I'm hungry again."

When he didn't respond, she left him to use the restroom. Some strands of her hair had come loose. It was smarter to just undo it and brush it out. Before he brought their dinner, she pulled out the pillows and propped them against the headboard. After taking off her sandals, she reached for the remote and got up on the bed. Before long Antonio walked in carrying a tray.

"Put it here between us." She patted the center of the bed.

"The steward still won't breathe a word of where we're going." He put the tray down. Sandwiches and salad.

"Loyal to the end." She smiled at him. "In the meantime this looks good."

"I think so too." He joined her on the bed and they began to eat.

"Do you mind if we talk? We haven't discussed how we're going to live. In the fairy tales the prince takes his bride to his kingdom and they live happily ever after, but we never get to see *how* they live."

He smiled. "I have my own home in one wing of the palace. Our bedroom and living room overlook the Mediterranean. It's totally private and will be our home. My office is on the main floor adjoining my father's. My parents have their own suite. You've already visited Elena in her suite, which is in the other wing. But we're far enough apart to lead separate lives."

She poured them both more coffee, then sat back to drink hers. "Is it going to feel terribly strange bringing a wife into your world?"

He finished off the rest of his sandwich. "I thought it would. In fact, I couldn't comprehend it. But after being with you, I'll feel strange if you're not with me. I've discovered that I've slipped into the husband role faster than I would have thought and I'm enjoying every minute of it."

Christina studied him for a moment. "Today I feel like we're beginning to get to know each other and aren't afraid to be ourselves. That was my greatest fear, that you'd be different from the man I knew as Elena's brother. I've worried that in living with the man you've become, I'd feel invisible walls that kept us strangers. But I don't feel that way at all when I'm around you."

"That's good to hear. I have no idea if I'm easy to live with, Christina, and beg your forgiveness ahead of time."

A gentle laugh escaped her lips. "That goes for me too. So far I have no complaints. I hope you don't mind if I ask you a few more questions."

"Why would I mind? This is all new. You can ask me anything."

She put down her empty coffee cup. "Is Guido going to be your chief of staff when you take over?"

"At first, yes. But he's been loyal to my father for years and when he sees how I intend to rule the country, he may have trouble supporting me."

As he was lying in bed, he'd worried about how everything would go while he was away on his honeymoon. If something went wrong before the coronation, he wouldn't be there to smooth things over. His father's note said no phone, no TV or internet while they were on vacation. He'd never been without those things and couldn't comprehend it at the time.

"*I'll* support you, Antonio. I believe in the changes you're going to make."

He heard the fervor in her voice and smiled at her. She was too good to be true. "If things get bad, how would you like to be my new chief of staff?"

Christina broke into laughter. "Now, there's a thought. The media will claim that Princess Christina is running the show."

"Better you than anyone else I can think of. But seriously, let's not worry about the future of the monarchy today. Look—" He sat forward. "I know everything will be strange at first."

"Elena said your mother has her own personal maid. I don't want one, Antonio. I find it absurd to ask someone to fetch and carry when I'm perfectly capable of doing those things myself. And I'd like to cook for you, go shopping at the markets. I can balance homemaking with the time spent at the charity foundation office in town."

The more she talked, the more he liked the sound of it. "We're on the same wavelength. All the years I lived in the States I did most things myself and prefer it, so I get where you're coming from. We'll make this work."

Her silvery eyes glistened with unshed tears. "Thank you for being so understanding." When she spoke, her heart was in her eyes and it touched a part of his soul.

"Thank *you* for marrying me." He meant it with all his heart.

A shadow crossed over her face. "Antonio—if I'd told you I didn't want to get married when you called, what do you think you would have done?"

"I don't know. What saddens me is that you weren't sure I'd follow through and marry you. Christina, I swear not to do anything consciously to hurt you or bring you grief. Do you believe that?"

"Of course I do," she answered in a trembling voice. "Now I'll stop pestering you and hand you the remote. Here are half a dozen movies. Choose whichever one you want. I'm loving this.

"When we get back to Halencia, I'm afraid everything will change. Elena told me your father's daily schedule is horrendous, so I consider this time precious to have you all to myself. Tomorrow we'll reach our destination, so I'm taking advantage of the time to talk to you."

"You've always been so easy to be with, Christina. You still are." More than ever... He clicked the remote and flipped slowly through the titles so she could have time to choose.

"Stop!" she cried out. "*The African Queen* in Italian? Half of that film was filmed in the Congo!"

Antonio grinned. "I never saw it."

"I bet we have Elena to thank for this one." She smiled. "Trust her to find me a film I'd enjoy. Do you mind if we watch it?"

"Not at all. It will give me a feel for where you've lived and worked all these years."

"I never worked in the Congo. The Kikuyu tribe lives on the central highlands, but it doesn't matter. The part in the Congo is authentic. Just don't forget it's an old, old movie, Antonio."

He flashed her a smile that turned her heart over. "I like old if it's good."

"This is good. I promise."

Christina settled back to watch the film while she finished her sandwich. She could tell Antonio liked it. He kept asking questions as if he was truly interested. Maybe he was. But if she continued to wonder when his reactions were natural or made up to please her every time he spoke, their marriage didn't have a hope of succeeding.

"The actress is a redhead like you."

"The poor thing. She probably suffered a lot as a child."

"She became a movie star, Christina. It obviously didn't hurt her."

He lay back on the bed and slid his hand into her hair splayed on the pillow. He lifted some strands in his fingers. "I love your hair. It gleams like red gold and smells like citrus."

"My shampoo is called Lemon Orange Peel. When I'm in Africa I have to use a shampoo with no scent so the tsetse flies and mosquitoes won't zero in on me."

"You'd be a target all right. Do you love it there so much?"

"Yes."

"You're wonderful, you know that?"

Her eyes filled with telltale moisture.

His hand moved to her face. He traced the outline of her jaw with his fingers. "You have flawless skin and a mouth I need to kiss again." Without asking her permission his lips brushed hers over and over until he coaxed them apart and began drinking deeply.

A moan escaped her throat as she felt herself falling under his spell. He rolled her into his rock-hard body. A myriad of sensations attacked her as she felt him rub her back, urging her closer. With every stroke, her body continued to melt as the heat started building inside her, making her feverish. Antonio was taking her to a place she'd never been before.

She wasn't cognizant of the fasten-seatbelt sign flashing until the captain's voice came over the intercom. "We've started to experience turbulence. For your safety, you need to come forward and sit until we get through this."

On a groan Antonio released her, much more in control than she was. "Come on. Let's go." He got off the bed and helped her to her feet.

She couldn't believe how bumpy it had become and clung to him while they made their way out of the bedroom and down the hallway to the couches. Christina had so much trouble fastening her seat belt that Antonio did it for her and then fastened his own.

"It's going to be all right." He reached for her hand.

The incident didn't last long. When the sign went off, she undid her seat belt and got up before Antonio did. "It's late. If you don't mind, I'm going to get ready for bed. Last night I hardly slept and now I'm exhausted."

After he undid his seat belt, he stood up. "You go ahead. I'm going to have a chat with the captain and will see you in the morning." He put a hand behind her head and pressed a firm kiss to her mouth before releasing her. "Get a good sleep."

"You too," she whispered before walking back to the bedroom she'd just left. Her legs felt like mush, but this had nothing to do with the bumpy flight. The kiss he'd just given her was able to reduce her to a trembling bride. A little while ago she'd experienced the kind of passion that would have rendered her witless and breathless given another minute in his arms.

Frightened because she'd almost lost control, she showered and got ready for bed. Once under the covers she had a talk with herself. It *was* too soon in their marriage for the physical side to take over. She didn't doubt Antonio's intentions. He was doing his best to be a considerate husband. There was nothing wrong with that, not at all. But she wanted to know his possession and realized this was what she got for entering into a marriage of convenience.

I don't want to be his convenient bride.

Christina wanted him to make love to her because he was in love with her and couldn't live without her. She wanted Antonio in every way a woman wanted her husband. From the age of fifteen she'd been attracted to him. All it had taken was that kiss at the altar to turn her inside out.

What have you done to me, Antonio?

She closed her eyes, reeling from that torturous question until she fell into oblivion.

The next time she was aware of her surroundings, her watch indicated she'd slept ten hours. All in all, they'd been flying twenty hours with refueling stops she hadn't been aware of. That meant they were close to their unknown destination.

If Antonio had come to her in the night, she didn't know about it. Chances were he'd been exhausted too and needed sleep as much as she did. She threw off the covers and went to the bathroom to brush her teeth and arrange her hair back in a French twist.

The more she thought about it, the more she believed they were flying to a beach vacation. After some deliberation, she chose to put on a pair of white pants and toned it with a filmy white top of aqua swirls that looked like sea spray. The short sleeves and round neck made it summery. Once she'd put on lipstick, she packed her bag so it would be ready to carry off the jet.

Antonio must have had the same thoughts, because when she walked through the plane to the dining area, she discovered him dressed in white pants and a white crew-neck shirt with navy blue trim. His virility took her breath.

As she approached, he broke off talking to the steward. "I was just about to come and wake you for breakfast. We'll be landing pretty soon. I've been told we don't want to miss the view before we touch down."

"That sounds exciting. How did you sleep?" She sat down at one of the tables.

He took his place opposite her. "I don't think as well as you."

"I'm sorry."

"Don't be. I'm a restless sleeper when I travel. When we touched down to refuel, I got out of the jet to stretch my legs. I peeked in on you to see if you wanted some exercise too, but you were out like a light."

She felt Antonio's admiring gaze before the steward served them another delicious meal that started off with several types of chilled melon balls in a mint juice. "Mmm. This is awesome."

"I agree," he said, still eyeing her face and hair over his cup of cappuccino until she felt a fluttery sensation in her chest.

They ate healthy servings of eggs, bread and jam. If she ate like this for every meal, she'd quickly put on the weight she'd slowly lost over the past year.

The steward came to their table. "The pilot will be addressing you in a minute. When you're through eating, please take your seats in the front section. He'll start the descent, allowing you a bird's-eye view."

"Thank you," Antonio said, exchanging a silent glance with her. By tacit agreement, they got up from the table and walked forward to one of the couches, where they sat together and buckled up.

In a minute the fasten-seat-belt sign flashed and they heard the captain over the intercom. "Your Highness? Princess Christina? It's eleven a.m. Tahitian time."

"Tahiti—" she blurted in delight, provoking a smile from Antonio who reached for her hand.

"We'll be landing at the airport built on the island next to Bora Bora. From there you'll be taken by helicopter to a nearby island that is yours exclusively for the next four days. The sight you're about to see is one of the most glorious in the world. Start watching out the windows."

Christina felt the plane begin to descend. Pretty soon she saw a sight that was out of this world. The captain said, "Bora Bora has been described as an emerald set in a sea of turquoise blue with a surrounding necklace of translucent white water."

"Incredible!" she and Antonio cried at the same time.

"There are dark green islands farther out in the lagoon that face the mountain. This lagoon is three times the size of the land mass."

"Oh, I can't believe this beauty is real." She shook her head. "No wonder sailors from long ago dreamed of reaching Bora Bora."

"To the southeast you'll see a coral garden with waters swimming with manta rays, barracudas and sharks. You can watch them at their feeding time."

She turned to her husband. "I'm not sorry your parents gave us this beautiful gift, Antonio. They couldn't have planned a more glorious honeymoon retreat for us."

"You're right." He squeezed her hand.

The jet circled lower and before long they touched down. Antonio undid both their seat belts. "I'll grab our suitcases. What else?"

"My white purse on the dresser."

He nodded. "I'll be right back." His excitement matched hers. They'd come to paradise and couldn't wait to get out in it.

She walked toward the galley to thank the steward.

"It's been my pleasure, Princess."

Antonio caught up to her with her purse. The steward carried their cases to the entrance of the jet where their pilot was waiting. He shook his hand. "Thank you for a flawless flight."

"It has been an honor for me to serve you and the princess. There's a helicopter waiting to fly you to your private resort where every need will be met. In four days I'll be here to fly you back to Halencia. Enjoy your honeymoon."

She left the jet with Antonio following her and made her way to the helicopter. The pilot, an islander, greeted them warmly and explained they'd be flying to one of those dark green islands in the distance.

Christina sat in one of the backseats. The second Antonio joined her and buckled up, the rotors screamed to life and they lifted off, flying low over the aquamarine water. The pilot spoke to them over the mic.

"Welcome to Tahiti. The resort has heard

that the future king and queen of Halencia are our guests. Word has come that you are much beloved, Princess. No one else will disturb your vacation, but you have a staff to wait on you. Ask for anything."

"Thank you."

When she looked back at Antonio, he was staring at her. "Do you know everyone who meets you is so charmed by you that you have them eating out of your hand? I noticed it as we were walking down the aisle after the ceremony. All eyes and smiles were focused on you."

A blush seeped into her cheeks. "A bride is always the center of attention at a wedding. It's the way of things."

"But my bride is exceptional and loved by the people already. If I'm to gain any credibility with the country when I'm king, it will be because of you."

"Thank you, but you don't need to say things like that to me."

"Yes, I do." The sincerity in his voice convinced her.

Before she knew it, the pilot set down the helicopter on a stretch of the purest white beach she'd ever seen. Another man in shorts and T-shirt was there to take their bags.

"Welcome to Bora Bora, Your Highnesses. I'm Manu and will be serving you. If you want anything, it will be at your disposal. With the powerboat you can go where you wish to fish, scuba dive, hike. Anything you want."

They shook his hand and followed him to their resort. It turned out to be a massive island bungalow of traditional Polynesian design with a vaulted ceiling situated on stilts over their private lagoon of turquoise water. As they walked inside, the living room looked like a sumptuous palace suite with windows on all sides and glass floors throughout to watch the fish.

There were windows on all sides and two different sundecks facing Bora Bora with platforms so they could step off directly into the lagoon.

Outside were oversize chairs and more glass floor panels. Manu showed them the dining room and kitchen with a refrigerator stocked with snacks and drinks. "There's food here to enjoy inside or to make a picnic. The spacious bathroom has two tubs and walk-in showers."

They followed him to the fabulous bedroom, also with a vaulted ceiling, where he put down their cases. Then he showed them out to one of the platforms. "The powerboat is ready and filled to capacity to take you where you want. Come with me to the other platform."

They followed him. "You have your own two-seater kayak, snorkeling equipment, rubber rafts, whatever you want including towels and sunscreen. The lagoon water is eighty degrees and the nighttime temperature is the same."

Warmer than a bathtub?

Christina marveled that everything you could ever want had been provided. She thanked Elena silently for taking her to buy some swimming suits.

"I'll be the person waiting on you. Pick up the phone to order your food or when you need clothes washed or ironed. There's one in the living room and another one in the bedroom. There's no internet, no television. If there's an emergency, you call me on the house phone and I'll take care of it. Can I answer any questions?"

"Not right now." Antonio shook his hand. "Thank you, Manu."

After the islander disappeared, she looked around in wonder. "All of this just for us?" she murmured to her husband. "Only a king could afford to pay the resort enough money to keep the world away."

He chuckled and turned to her. "What do you want to do first?"

"Let's unpack and then go for a swim. That water is calling to me."

Antonio couldn't help but admit that this had to be the ultimate getaway. His parents had gone over-the-top on this one, but he'd promised Christina they'd enjoy this outrageous luxury and not count the cost.

It didn't take long to put their things in closets and drawers. Then she disappeared in the bathroom. While she was out of sight he changed into his boxer-style black bathing trunks. Wanting to create a mood, he went into the living room and searched in the entertainment center for the radio.

When he turned it on, he got Tahitian

music, exactly what he wanted. There was a switch that said Outside. He flipped it and suddenly they were surrounded with island music that no doubt could be heard out on the beach.

A smiling Christina came hurrying in wearing a lacy peach-colored beach robe over what looked like a darker peach bikini. Her gorgeous long legs took his breath away. "That's such romantic music, I think I'm dreaming all this."

"Fun, isn't it? Let's go try out the water."

He opened the door that led to the platform off the living room. She leaned over the railing to look down at the water. "It's clear as crystal." When she reached the edge of the platform, she removed her beach coat and put it over the railing.

"Wait, Christina. You need some sunscreen or you'll pick up a bad sunburn."

"You're right."

"I'll get it." He went over to the basket and brought it to her. "I'll put some on your back and shoulders."

She turned her back toward him without hesitation. Her skin felt like satin and he loved rubbing the cream over her. The legitimate excuse to touch her made him wish he didn't have to stop. Summoning all the self-control he could muster, he handed her the tube so she could do the rest herself.

"Thank you," she said in a shaky voice. "Now it's my turn to put some on you, although you're already tanned."

He longed to feel her hands on him. His pulse throbbed as he felt her spread the cream over his shoulders and back. After putting the tube on the railing, she jumped in the shallow water and shrieked with joy.

"Oh, Antonio— This is divine!" She splashed the water with her hands and laughed in delight before lying back while her legs did the work of keeping her afloat.

One look at her and he couldn't reach her soon enough. Bathtub was right. The temperature here stayed around eighty day and night. He swam up next to her, infected by her sounds of excitement. With the Polynesian music filling the air, they were like children who'd discovered the fount of pure pleasure.

Together they moved out deeper into the blue lagoon. He swam under and around her.

The glimpses of her exquisitely molded body set his heart pounding.

"Look at that darling little sea turtle!"

Spectacular as it was, he would rather look at her. As they trod water, they caught sight of other types of small fish including a clown fish with orange and white stripes. One discovery turned into another. They played and darted through the water for several hours, concocting silly games to identify the fish they saw. Her prowess as a swimmer was going to make this the adventure of a lifetime.

Since there was no one else around, Antonio felt as if they were the last two people on earth...or the first. Adam and Eve?

He loved the idea of it, loved being with her like this where her guard was down. Her sense of fun was already making this trip unforgettable. "What do you say we go back and drink something icy cold while we sunbathe on the lounge chairs?"

"That sounds perfect. I'll race you back."

Together they did the crawl. He slowed his pace to stay even with her. When they reached the platform he climbed up first, then helped her. She put on her beach robe and headed for one of the loungers.

"I'll order some drinks and be right back."

"No alcohol for me. Even a little wine can give me a headache."

"Did you suffer from one on our wedding night?"

"No, because I only sipped a little, but I know to be careful."

That was something he didn't know. He rarely drank himself and was pleased to learn she didn't care about it. His parents constantly overindulged.

A few minutes later and Manu appeared with two frosted glasses of juice topped with a flower.

"I could get used to this in a hurry," Christina commented after they'd given him their order for dinner and were alone again. Antonio handed her some of the brochures from the table in the living room. He looked over one, but would study the rest of them later. Right now he was content to study her and look at the white clouds moving slowly across the sky.

He finished his drink. "It'll be several hours before dinner, but it's already late in the day. How would you like to go exploring in the powerboat? We'll follow the directions in that brochure and make our plans for tomorrow."

"That's exactly what I want to do. While we were descending in the plane, I longed to spend more time just to get acquainted with this glorious place."

A few minutes later they undid the ropes and Antonio idled them out into the lagoon. He reached into one of the lockers. "Here—put this lifesaving belt on." He handed it to her.

"But the water isn't that deep."

"It doesn't matter. If we got into trouble, you'd be glad of it."

"I'll wear it if you wear one too."

"Nag, nag." But he smiled as he put one on.

"Now that I think about it, can you imagine the media storm if we had an accident and word got out that the future king and queen of Halencia had almost drowned because they hadn't been wearing preservers? People would wonder what kind of ruler they had."

He chuckled. "Point taken. It would never do."

Off Point Matira they came across a group

of huge manta rays. There were spotted and gray rays. Antonio swam near their boat while they watched in fascination.

"We should be marine biologists," she exclaimed. "Just think, we could come out to places like this and spend all day long for weeks on end."

Antonio nodded. "Being out here, you can understand the appeal for that kind of work. Are you interested in watching the locals feed the sharks? We're not far from there."

"I guess it's safe or they wouldn't advertise it, but I think I'll want to stay in the boat."

He drove them to the spot where the local divers stood chest deep in the water. Four-and five-foot sharks circled around them to get their food.

"That's scary to me," Christina said. "I've changed my mind about being a biologist."

"Instead you'd rather be in Kenya where you can be dragged off by a lion."

"No—" She grinned at him.

For their last destination they took off and headed for the coral garden, an underwater park southwest of Bora Bora Island. For an hour they were spellbound by the amount of colorful fish and coral. Like an excited child she squealed over the varieties.

"I'm going to take a quick dip before we head back."

Antonio couldn't have stopped her. She was too anxious to get closer. Off came her belt and she lowered herself in the water. The sight of her going underwater made him nervous. He watched her like a hawk. To his relief she came back up a few minutes later, but she looked distressed.

"I stepped on something, but I don't know what."

Diavolo. "Does it sting?"

"No. It's just kind of sore on the pad of my foot."

Antonio leaned over and helped her into the boat. He set her down on the banquette so he could inspect it. "You made contact with a sea urchin, but luckily I only see two spines." *Thank heaven.* "They'll need to come out. Keep your leg on the banquette and I'll get us back home." He wrapped the life belt around her, kissed her lips and got behind the wheel.

"Do you think it's serious?"

"No. I once got a whole foot full of them,

but I was fine. Still, we'll ask the doctor to check you."

"Oh no—I didn't mean for this to happen."

"Accidents can happen anytime in the water, as you reminded me."

The sky was darkening fast. He was glad when they reached their island. After tying up the boat, he undid the life belts and carried her from the deck into their bedroom.

After setting her down on top of the bed, he phoned Manu and asked for a doctor to come. "I'll get you some ibuprofen after we've talked to the doctor."

"Will you carry me to the bathroom? I need to get out of my suit and into a robe."

"Of course." He lifted her in his arms once more and let her hang on to him while he reached for her robe hanging on the door. "Can I help you?"

"I'll be all right." He waited until she said she was ready, and then he carried her back to the bed. In another moment he heard Manu's voice coming from the main entrance. "The doctor is here."

"Will you show him into the bedroom, Manu?"

Within seconds the two men came in. "Princess Christina? This is Dr. Ulani."

He brought his bag with him. "Thank you for coming, Doctor. As you can see, my wife stepped on a sea urchin. She's in pain."

"Hush, Antonio. It's not that bad at all. More of a discomfort."

The native doctor smiled. "Accidents like this happen every day, even to someone like Your Highness. Let me check your foot. I'll try not to add to your pain."

Antonio placed a chair for him to sit while he worked on her. Relieved as he was that she was getting medical attention, it suddenly hit him how frightened he'd been when she first surfaced. In very little time she'd become so important to him that he couldn't bear the thought of anything truly serious being wrong with her.

The doctor opened his bag and proceeded to get rid of the two spines. He put ointment on the sores and a dressing. "You'll be fine tomorrow. Just make sure you wear some kind of shoe in the water if you're not snorkeling with fins. I'll give you a tablet for you to sleep that will kill the pain. Tomorrow if you're still too sore, take some ibuprofen."

"Thank you so much. It feels better already."

"It's a privilege to help you, Princess." When he'd finished, he stood up. "Take care, now."

"I'll make sure of it," Antonio muttered. He shouldn't have let her slip into the water like that. The action had caught him off guard.

"Here's the pill. Tomorrow you can take off the dressing."

Antonio walked him out to the living room. "I can't tell you how grateful I am you came."

"It is my pleasure to wait on the future king and queen of Halencia. Our people are aware of your presence here and they are delighted. Don't hesitate to get hold of me through Manu if you are alarmed by anything."

Manu stood by. "You want your dinner in the bedroom, Your Highness?"

"Yes. Thank you. Will you bring a glass of water so she can take her medicine?"

He nodded and hurried to the kitchen. Antonio headed back to the bedroom. "Christina? It's my fault you got hurt this evening."

"Nonsense. I wasn't thinking. When I saw those fish, I just had to get in closer."

"Please tell me you'll give me a heads-up next time before you do a disappearing act."

His mermaid was resting against the headboard with a sore foot. "I'm sorry to be the one at fault for not having the sense to get in the water prepared. But, Antonio, you don't have to try to be perfect with someone as imperfect as I am. I did a stupid thing, but the situation really is funny, don't you think? Your parents planning for every contingency to bring us joy? And I blew it. At least for tonight. Now you have to give me my medicine and be stuck with your ball and chain until morning."

"Don't say that! Not ever! I don't feel that way about you and never could. Promise me!" He sounded truly upset.

"I promise," she said as Manu appeared with their dinner. Antonio thanked him and put the tray of food on the side of the bed next to her. He handed her the glass of water and the pill. "Take this first."

After she did his bidding, he sat in the chair the doctor had used and they ate their dinner. He heard her sigh.

"It's another beautiful night, so balmy. I'd wanted to go walking on the beach with you."

"We'll do that tomorrow night. For now, you need to try and fall asleep."

"You won't leave me?" Her eyes beseeched him.

"As if I would," he murmured, experiencing a hard tug of emotion. It came to him that his new wife had become of vital importance to him. "I'll join you as soon as I change out of my swimming suit."

"Good. Don't be long."

Christina, Christina.

He put the tray on the table and went into the bathroom to change. After putting on a robe, he turned out the lights, then got into bed beside her. The pill must have been powerful, because her eyelids were drooping. Antonio rolled her into him and she let out a deep sigh. Soon she was asleep. Before long, oblivion took over.

Around six in the morning he felt the bed move. She'd gotten up to use the bathroom.

He eyed her through sleep-filled eyes. When she returned he said, "How's the pain?"

"There's hardly any at all. I can walk fine as long as I'm careful."

"That's wonderful news. Come back to bed and rest that foot some more. It's still early."

CHAPTER SIX

CHRISTINA EYED HER HUSBAND, who'd kept a vigil over her all night. She got back in bed, lying on her side so she could watch him sleep. He was such a gorgeous man. Dawn was sneaking into the bedroom with the morning breeze. Through the open windows she could see the unique shape of the mountains on Bora Bora. If she could be anywhere in the world, she wanted to be right here with the man she'd married.

When next she came awake, she found herself the object of Antonio's blue gaze. She propped her head up with her hand. "How long have you been awake?"

"Long enough to watch my lovely wife. You've been sleeping so peacefully."

Without hesitation he leaned over to kiss

her. "Good morning, *esposa mia*. I dreamed about kissing you all night long."

"I had the same dream."

Before she could blink he put his arm around her and kissed her deeply, not letting her go until she had to breathe.

He sighed. "I needed that."

"I'm pretty sure you need something else after taking care of me all night. I'll ring Manu to bring our breakfast tray." She reached for the phone and put in their order. After hanging up, she turned to her husband.

"How did you know?"

"That you're starving?" she quipped. "I'm hungry too."

He raised himself up and leaned over her. "You have no idea how beautiful you are, do you? I could eat you up."

But at that moment Manu appeared at the door. "Shall I put your breakfast on the table?"

"No, Manu," Antonio said. "I think we'll have it right here in bed."

The other man smiled and set it on the end of the bed before making a discreet departure.

She smiled at her husband. "We're spoiled rotten. You know that."

He moved to put the tray between them. Christina propped her head with a couple of pillows and bit into a croissant. "If the famous French impressionist Gauguin were here to paint us, he'd entitle it *Petit Déjeuner au Lit Tahitien*."

His lips twitched. "Breakfast in a Tahitian bed is far too mundane. I think a more appropriate title would be *Le Mari Amoureux*."

The Amorous Husband? Christina laughed to cover the quiver that ran through her. She'd forgotten he'd attended a French/Swiss boarding school too and was fluent in French besides Halencian, Italian, English and Spanish.

"What do you want to do today?"

"I'm up for anything."

"Honestly?"

"My foot doesn't hurt and I don't want us to miss out on anything while we're here. We don't have that much time before we have to go back."

"I don't want to go back."

Her pulse raced. "Neither do I."

"What do you say we take out the kayak and just paddle around for fun?"

"That sounds perfect. I'll get my suit on and wear a T-shirt so I don't pick up any more sun on my shoulders." With a kiss to his jaw, she slid out of bed. "I'll be back in a minute."

He'd been worried about that. The need to touch her was growing. A bad case of sunburn could make her feel miserable for several days. Relieved that her foot was healing well, he got excited to think about spending another glorious day with her. It was pure selfishness on his part to want her able to do everything with him waking or sleeping.

There was only one bed, but a number of couches. He had no intention of sleeping on a couch or a sun lounger tonight. He wanted his wife in that oversize bed clinging to him while the scented breeze from Bora Bora wafted through their bedroom.

"Antonio? I'm ready when you are."

He looked up to see her standing there with a white T-shirt pulled over her suit. "I'm glad you're wearing your tennis shoes."

There was no doubt his bride had one of the most beautiful faces and bodies he'd ever seen, starting with her glorious hair. She'd fastened it on top with a clip. He wanted to reach up and pull her down to him, but right now it was important they keep having fun while breaking down walls.

Levering himself out of bed, he hurried to the bathroom to put on his trunks. Then he joined her at the edge of the platform. The Sevylor inflatable plastic kayak had been secured to the post with cords. Once they were undone he reached down to hand her a belt life preserver. While she put hers on, he fastened his.

"I'll go first." After getting in the front seat, he held out his hands to her and eased her into the backseat.

"Ooh—" She laughed. "It's tippy. I'm used to a canoe."

"You'll soon get the hang of it."

They unloosened their oars and started paddling. He led them around in circles to get her used to the motion. Over his shoulder he said, "According to the brochure, there's no surf here because of the reef across the lagoon. When you're ready, we'll head out to that other island in the distance."

"I can see you're an old pro at this."

"During my boarding school days in Lausanne, some friends that my parents didn't approve of flew home with me on breaks. We'd go kayaking around Halencia on weekends. But as you know, the Mediterranean can be choppy when the wind comes up. This lagoon is like glass in comparison."

They started paddling together and headed out. "I wonder if I ever saw you out there during the few times I came home from boarding school."

"I've been wondering the same thing myself. Do you believe in destiny, Christina?"

"To be honest, until I received the phone call from you that we were really getting married, I believed that I was meant to—" She broke off abruptly. "Oh, it doesn't matter what I believed."

He stopped paddling and turned to look at her. "Tell me. I want to know."

She shook her head. "If I told you, you'd see me as a pitiful creature who feels sorry for herself."

"You're anything but pitiful. I want to know what you were going to say."

Christina rested her oar. She cast her gaze toward Bora Bora. "My parents didn't want me, Antonio. They really didn't. The only genuine love I felt came from my great-aunt Sofia, but I wasn't her daughter and didn't see her very often.

"I believed it was my lot always to live on the outside of their lives. This became evident when they didn't put up a fuss about my working in Africa. I was crushed when they sounded happy about my doing charity work there. They didn't miss me, not at all. Marusha's parents have been more like parents to me than anyone."

Her suffering had to be infinite. "That's tragic about your parents."

"I was afraid you'd say that, but I don't want you to feel sorry for me. They were warmer to me at the wedding, especially Mother. You asked for the truth and I've told you. As for believing in destiny, despite my pain, I was happy with my life in Africa and decided I'd probably live there forever. The ability to help other people brought me a lot of peace I hadn't known before."

"Until I turned your world upside down," he bit out in self-deprecation.

"It wasn't just you, Antonio. Elena had already become family to me. When she got into real trouble, I felt her pain. Like you, she led a life of isolation being royal. I can understand why she took up with guys from my world. In your own way, you and Elena have led a life of loneliness. It's a strange world you two inhabit and always will be. But I was lucky enough to be the friend Elena let in. If I could have had a sister, I would have wanted her."

"You're very perceptive, Christina. I originally went to San Francisco to learn business. It was there I worked with normal people. Zach became a true friend and I enjoyed it so much I didn't want to go home. My parents' lifestyle was a personal embarrassment to me. But when I heard of the trouble Elena was in, I couldn't turn my back on her. Forgive me for using you."

"By phoning you, I used you too," Christina came back. "Did you really have a choice to do anything but try to draw the paparazzi's attention away from her? I was the perfect person to help. After all, we were an unlikely threesome, yet no one knew me or knew about me. What I want to know is, why didn't you break off our engagement a few years later and ask the woman you loved to marry you?"

His jaw hardened. "I wouldn't have done that to you."

"You see what I mean?"

Her sad smile pierced him.

"You tried to be like everyone else, but in the end, the prince in you dominated your will. The princess in Elena let you fall on your sword because you were both born to royalty and knew your duty. She wanted you to be king one day.

"Before I phoned you, did you know she wanted to admit everything to the police and take the blame so there'd be no reflection on you or your family? But I wouldn't let her. I told her I was going to phone you because I knew you could fix things and you found a way."

"Which involved you." His voice throbbed. His emotions hovered near the surface. "Let me ask you a question. Why didn't you tell me to go to hell when I called you to give you the wedding date? You would have had every right."

She breathed in deeply. "Because your royal dust had blown on me years before.

I'm not a Halencian for nothing. My country means everything to me. The engagement we entered into was very bizarre, but it made a strange kind of sense. In fact, the only kind of sense that would satisfy the people.

"I'm positive it would have been hard for them to accept your marriage to a woman from a different nationality as you pointed out. But if you'd wanted it badly enough, you could have made it happen."

He eyed her for a moment. "When it came down to it, I didn't want her badly enough to break my commitment to you."

"Thank you for saying that. I want you to know I'm not sorry, Antonio."

His heart skipped a beat. "Do you honestly mean it? Even though it meant ending an important relationship with the doctor you met in Kenya?"

"It wasn't that important. I didn't want to break my commitment to you either. You and Elena have trod a treacherous path all your lives. You always will because you were born to the House of L'Accardi.

"Elena and I were friends from the age of fifteen. I knew her sorrows. She bore mine. Her greatest fear was that you might end up living in California one day and giving up the throne so she would have to be queen. That was one of her greatest nightmares."

Good heavens. So much had gone on that he hadn't known about behind the scenes because of his selfishness in pursuing his own dream. "I didn't realize…"

"How could you if she never said any-thing? At our reception, Elena acted so happy we got married that she could hardly contain herself." Even though there was still something she seemed to be holding back.

"Her happiness went much deeper than that because it meant she wasn't going to lose the best friend she's ever had."

Christina flashed a full, radiant smile at him, stunning him. "Now she's got both of us and our threesome can go on forever."

Forever.

Antonio turned around and started paddling again. There'd been a time when the thought of being married forever stuck in his throat. But no longer. When they returned to the hut, Manu had served their dinner on the deck.

"Tonight you are eating freshly caught

mahimahi with coconut rice and mango salsa."

"It looks fantastic, Manu."

After he left them alone Christina said, "They've gone all out for us. Now I know the true meaning of being treated like a king."

His blue eyes glinted with amusement as they sat down to eat.

Christina took her first bite. "The fish is out of this world."

"This is Bora Bora mahimahi," he quipped. "We won't be getting anything this good in Halencia. If I could put off the coronation for a while, I'd like us to stay here for a month at least! I'm thinking our first-year anniversary. What do you say?"

"But we'll fly commercial. And we'll stay in a little bungalow over the water and play tourist like everyone else."

"And climb the mountain and scuba dive. Have you ever been?"

"No."

"Then you've got to take lessons. I'll go with you."

"You mean you'll take time out of your busy day?"

"You'll need a buddy. I don't want anyone else buddying up with *my* wife."

The possessive tone in his voice thrilled her.

Once dinner was over Christina showered and washed her hair. After toweling it, she used the blow dryer until it swished against her shoulders. She put on a pale lemon-colored nightgown. Her skin had picked up some sun, adding color to her complexion. To her relief her injury was barely noticeable.

Her lamp was the only light on in the room. There were more brochures for her to read on the side table, but she wasn't ready for bed yet. Antonio had turned on more romantic music. The thought of him made her heart thump out of control. She'd just spent the most heavenly day of her life with the man who was now her husband.

Before long he came into the bedroom wearing a robe. Without a shirt he had an amazing male physique with a dusting of dark hair on his chest. Her mouth went dry just looking at him. When he came closer, she could smell the soap he'd used in the shower. "The night is calling to us. Let's go out on the deck. I want to dance with you."

He grasped her hand and they walked out into the balmy night. Christina gasped softly to see millions of stars overhead. "Antonio—have you ever seen the heavens this alive? I just saw a shooting star."

"We don't need a telescope when the universe seems so close. It's even in your eyes. They are shimmering like newly minted silver. Combined with the red gold of your hair, you're an amazing sight. A new heavenly body to light up this unforgettable night."

His words overwhelmed her before he wrapped his arms around her and started dancing with her. Not the kind of dancing they did at the reception. This was slow dancing. She melted into him. The night had seduced her. There was a fragrance in the air from the flowers on the deck that intoxicated her. Being held against his hard body like this was pure revelation.

Her womanhood had come alive in his arms. She liked being taller because their bodies fit together. He'd buried his face in her hair. She could feel the warmth of his breath, tantalizing her because she longed to feel his mouth on hers. On their wedding night she'd thought the fantasy was over. How could she have known they would come to this paradise where she was finding rapture beyond her dreams?

"Give me your mouth, Christina," he murmured. "I'm aching for you."

She had the same ache and lifted her head. Their mouths met and they kissed for a long time, giving and taking, back and forth. She clung to him, needing the pleasure he gave her with every caress of his hands roaming over her back. When he moved his mouth lower, she moaned as he slowly kissed her neck and throat. Everywhere his lips touched, it brought heat that spread through her body like fire.

Without her realizing it, he'd danced them back inside. Then he swept her into his arms and followed her down on the bed. "I could eat you alive," he whispered against her lips, and once again Christina was consumed by his kiss, hot with desire. A *husband's* desire. She hadn't known it could be like this.

"*Bellissima?* Tell me something. Have you ever been to bed with a man?"

The question jolted her. "No. Does my in-experience show so much?"

"Not at all. But I worried that if I'm the first man to make love to you, then I don't want to rush you into anything. You're so sweet, Christina. I didn't need Elena to tell me just how sweet you really are. I want our first time to be everything for you."

"Everything has been perfect so far," she whispered, fearing something had to be lacking in her for him to bring it up. When he didn't say anything, she eased away a little, but he drew her to him with her back resting against his chest.

"I'm glad, but I want to give you time to get used to me. Until you're truly ready, let's simply hold each other tonight. If I'd gone to Africa to see you, this is what we would have done. We have the rest of our lives and don't need to be in a hurry." He kissed her neck. "This is heavenly, you know? You smell and feel divine to me."

To be held in his arms was heavenly, but little did he know she *was* ready! Though she loved him for trying to make their first time perfect, she was dying inside. Still, by his determination to ease her into marriage, it showed a tender side of his nature that proved what a wonderful man she'd married. How many men would care enough about their brides' feelings to go to these lengths?

"This has been my idea of heaven, Antonio. I can't wait until tomorrow." Maybe tomorrow night he'd realize she didn't want to wait a second longer.

When she awakened the next morning, she discovered her husband fast asleep. They'd slept late. Christina slid out of bed without disturbing him and rushed into the kitchen to phone Manu and order breakfast. Then she showered to get ready for the day.

With that accomplished she put on another bikini. This one had an apple-green flutter top. Both she and Elena had loved the crocheted look of the top and bottom overlying a white lining. It was more modest than many of the suits.

Since they'd probably be out in the water most of the day, she decided the best thing to do with her hair was to sweep it on top and secure it with her tortoiseshell clip. She removed her gold studs and put on a pair of tiny earrings the shape of half-moons in a green that matched her bikini.

Before going in to Antonio, she threw on a lacy white beach jacket that fell to just below her thighs. Now she was ready to greet her husband. But when she entered the bedroom, he'd turned onto his stomach and was still out for the count. Only a sheet covered his lower half. What a fabulous-looking man! She was still pinching herself to believe he was her husband.

He would need a shave, but she loved the shadow on his hard jaw. He looks were so arresting that his state of dress or his grooming didn't matter. She'd loved the handsome eighteen-year-old prince. But over the years he'd grown into a breathtaking man no woman could be immune to.

While she sat feasting her eyes on him, she heard sounds coming from the kitchen. She got up from the side of the bed and went back to bring him their breakfast tray. She brought it in and put it on the end of the bed.

The aroma of the coffee must have awakened him. He turned on his side and opened his eyes. Between the dark fringe of his lashes, their brilliant blue color stole her breath. Antonio raised himself up on one elbow. "Well, what do we have here? Could it be the nymph from the fountain holding the seashell?"

She loved the imagery. He'd noticed the fountain sculpture in the courtyard in front of the palazzo. "Yes, sire." His eyes darkened with emotion. "I'm here with your breakfast. Your wife told me you would awaken with a huge appetite."

"My wife told you that? Her exact words?"

"I never lie."

"Then will you tell her that spending the day with her yesterday was more than wonderful? But I'll tell her just how wonderful when we're alone again today. Those will be words for her ears only."

Christina couldn't prevent the blush that rose into her cheeks. "I'll be happy to do that after I've served you your breakfast." She got up and put the tray in front of him. "Do you wish me to leave? You have only to command me."

"Then I command you to bring that chair over to the side of the bed and we'll enjoy this food together."

She smiled secretly and moved it next to the bed. "Your wife won't mind?"

He flicked her an all-encompassing gaze.

"She might. A woman serving me breakfast who looks as gorgeous as you might worry, so I think we'll keep this moment to ourselves. How does that sound to you?"

She reached for a roll and bit into it. "You flatter me, sire."

"I haven't even started. That's quite an outfit you're wearing."

Christina drank some orange juice and reached for a strip of bacon. "You like it?"

"I can't keep my eyes off you. Do you serve all the men like that?"

"What men? You're the only one on this whole island."

He ate his food in record time. "That's good because if I found out otherwise, I'd have to confine you to a room in the palace where I have the only key."

Their conversation was getting sillier and sillier, but she loved it. She loved *him*.

"What are your plans for today, sire?"

"This and that."

"Does your wife know about that?"

His eyes narrowed on her mouth. "She'll find out."

"I see." Her heart jumped. "Well, if you've

finished your breakfast, I'll take the tray back to the kitchen."

"*Grazie*. When you see her, tell her I want her to come to me. *Now*. I don't like to be kept waiting."

She trembled as she reached for the tray. "*Si*, Your Highness."

The second his wife left the bedroom on those long, shapely legs, Antonio headed for the shower and freshened up. Since she'd already put on her bikini, he pulled on a fresh pair of white bathing trunks. When he'd told her last night he could eat her alive, he hadn't been kidding.

"*Ciao*, Antonio." She was looking at one of the brochures while waiting for him.

"I understood you wanted to see me?" Her smile curved so seductively he wanted to throw her on the bed and stay there all day, but he resisted the urge. She was a fetching siren. Who would have guessed?

"How would you like to go to the nearby island with the waterfall? Manu says it's a short hike, but worth it if you're wearing tennis shoes."

"I love hikes. I did it all over Switzerland and Kenya."

She was amazing. "Manu told me it's off-limits to everyone else while we're here on our honeymoon."

Her eyes lit up. "A whole island to ourselves? Let's do it! I'll pack us some food so we don't have to come back for dinner."

"Why not pack enough food in case we want to stay there overnight?"

"You mean sleep by the waterfall?"

He smiled at her. It was all he could think about. "Why not? Haven't you ever wondered what it would be like to be Tarzan and Jane?"

She chuckled in response. "Yes. Many times."

"We'll take the speedboat."

With their day decided, they packed things in the backpacks supplied by the resort, including light blankets, food and water. Antonio rang Manu to let him know where they were going. Then they left their retreat and took off for one of the dark green islands they could see in the distance that was taller than the others.

"The lagoon never changes, Antonio. It's

like eternal beauty all the time. I've never been this excited to do anything."

She was reading his mind. They skimmed across the gorgeous blue water before reaching the white beach. Once they'd drunk some bottled water, they headed for the trail Manu said would be visible. Sure enough, they found it and started up the incline.

"The vegetation is so lush!" she exclaimed.

"Our own rain forest." Their gazes clung before they got going on their trek. It took them less time to reach their destination than to have kayaked over there. Flowers grew in abundance. They spotted terns and swallows. The water came down in a stream, small at first, then widening before they reached the waterfall itself.

"Oh, Antonio—it reminds me of a waterfall scene in an old movie I once saw, but I think it was filmed in Hawaii."

"This is as primitive as it gets." He helped her off with her pack and gave her a long kiss. Then he removed his.

"Isn't that spray marvelous? Look up there. If we can get on those rocks, we can ride the water down to the pool," she said.

"Let me test the depth of it first." He walked over to the edge and waded in the swirling water. He discovered that after a few steps there was a drop-off, but when he swam underwater he found it was only about twenty feet deep. When he emerged, he waved to her. "Come on in. It's safe but a little cooler than the lagoon. Keep your tennis shoes on."

For several hours they played in the water like children. Eventually they climbed up the side to reach the spot where the water from the mountain poured over the top of the rocks. He turned to his wife. "Shall we do it?"

"Yes."

"Scared?"

"Terrified."

"Take my hand."

Together they moved onto the slippery rocks and before long the strength of the waterfall washed over them, plunging them down into the pool. Christina came up laughing. "Oh, Antonio—talk about a rush! This just couldn't be real."

He swam to her and kissed her over and over again while keeping them afloat. "We've found paradise, *innamorata*. How about one more jump, and then we'll make camp for the night?"

Once again they hiked up the side to the top. Before they went out on the rocks, he plucked a white flower with a gardenia scent, growing on a nearby vine. He tucked it behind her ear. "Now you're my Polynesian princess."

Her eyes wandered over him. "I don't ever want to go home."

"Then we won't." He grabbed her hand and they inched their way onto the rocks until the force of the water took them over the edge. It was like free-falling into space until the water caught them and brought them to the surface.

Together they swam to the edge of the pool where they'd left their packs. He helped her out of the water and they proceeded to set up camp. After they'd made their bed, they put out the food. The exertion had made them hungry. They sat across from each other and ate to their hearts' content.

He finally stretched. "I've never felt so good, never tasted food so good, never been with anyone I enjoyed more. In truth, I've never been this happy in my life."

"I feel the same way," she responded. "I want it to last, but I know it's not going to."

He shook his head. "Shh. Don't spoil this heavenly evening. We have two more days and nights ahead of us."

"You're right."

"You've lost your gardenia. I'm going to pick another one." He got up and walked a ways until he found one. When he returned, he hunkered down next to her and put it behind her ear. "This is how I'm always going to remember you."

Antonio couldn't wait to get close to her again and cleaned up their picnic. When everything had been put away, she started to leave, but he caught her by the ankle. "Stay with me."

"I was just going to get out of my bathing suit."

"But I want to hold you first." He pulled her down and rolled onto his side so he could look at her. "I've been waiting all day for tonight to come."

"So have I." Her voice throbbed.

He pulled her into him and claimed her

luscious mouth that had given him a heart attack last night. "You could have no idea how much I want you. Love me, Christina. I need you."

"Would it shock you if I told I wanted you to love me on our wedding night?" she admitted against his throat.

He let out a slight groan. "Why didn't you tell me?"

"I was afraid you would think I was too eager. I decided you needed time."

Laughter broke from him. When he looked down at her, those fabulous silvery eyes were smiling. "I think that from here on out we each need to stop worrying about what the other one is thinking, and do more doing."

"I couldn't agree more. You drove me crazy on the way over in the jet."

"Maybe that was a good thing," he teased, kissing every feature on her face.

"It was painful!"

"Tesora mia," he cried in a husky voice before starting to devour her. "I love your honesty. Come here to me."

Christina melted in his arms and kissed

him with the kind of passion he'd never imagined to find in this marriage. His heart jumped to realize he had such a loving, demonstrative wife.

CHAPTER SEVEN

ANTONIO HAD CALLED her his treasure. Christina felt cherished and desirable. His hunger aroused her to the depth of her being. This was her husband bringing her to life, shocking her, thrilling her as they found new ways to worship each other with their bodies.

His long legs trapped hers. "Why did I wait four years?"

She couldn't have answered him if she'd wanted to. Enthralled by the things he was doing to her, Christina was too consumed by her own hunger for him. Like the spiral constellations lighting the canopy above, he sent her spiraling into another realm of existence. Throughout the hours of the night they loved fully until they finally fell asleep, only temporarily sated.

After their passion-filled night of ecstasy,

she couldn't believe they were still on earth. During the night he'd swept her to a different place, so intimate she'd wanted to stay on that sphere of euphoria forever.

She lay there wondering if last night's lovemaking had resulted in a baby. Stranger things had happened to other women. She suddenly realized that she wanted his baby so badly she could hardly stand it.

Heat washed over her to remember what had happened between them last night. Christina wasn't sorry that he hadn't made love to her at first. Far from it. Last night had been magical.

Taking great care not to wake her husband *and* lover, she lay there looking at him. The sun was already high in the morning sky. They'd slept in late again, but it didn't matter.

Oh, Antonio—I love you so much, you have no idea.

Antonio heard his wife sigh and glanced at her in sleep. She was the most unselfish lover he could ever have imagined. Last night she'd made him feel totally alive. Whole. When had he ever felt like this? Long after the stars had come out, they'd made love again and early this morning, again. He'd found paradise with her.

The next time he had cognizance of his surroundings, the sun was high in the sky. His wife lay on her side facing him. For a while he lay there studying her, then got to his feet and took a dip in the pool before pulling on his bathing trunks. He opened the backpack to get out some rolls and fruit. They'd need more food to stay on this island. He drank half a bottle of water while he ate.

She must have heard him and opened her eyes. "Oh—you're up!"

"Just barely. Loving you has given me a ferocious appetite."

She laughed. "I'm getting up, but you'll have to turn your head."

"Why?" he teased.

Christina blushed beautifully. "You know why."

"I'm your husband."

"I know, but—"

"All right. I'll close my eyes, but I'll give you to the count of ten to reach the water before I open them again."

"Antonio—" she squealed.

"One, two." He could hear the blanket rustle before she got up. A second later he heard water splashing and turned to watch her treading water. "You see? You made it."

"If you'll please put my bikini near the water and turn around, I'll get dressed."

Antonio's deep laughter resounded through the forest. She could feel it reverberate inside her. "Anything to oblige." He did her bidding. "I hate to tell you this, but the water is so transparent I can see you perfectly."

"You're no gentleman to say that to me."

"Is that what you thought I was?" he mocked before turning his back.

She climbed out and dressed as fast as she could. When she reached him, he crushed her in his arms and gave her a kiss to die for. Then he handed her food and drink.

"Thank you."

"You're welcome."

"I wish we could stay here longer. Last night—" Her voice caught.

Their eyes met. "Last night will be burned in my memory forever, *tesora*."

"Mine too." She finished eating and started putting everything in their packs.

He worked with her. "Are you about ready?"

"Yes."

After slipping on their tennis shoes, they started down the trail to the beach. In some parts she walked behind him, enjoying the play of muscle across his back and shoulders. Antonio had great legs for a man. In fact, there wasn't a part of him that wasn't perfect.

They reached the boat and loaded it. Christina helped him push it into the water, and then he helped ease her up and in before he took his place at the front. Before they took off across the lagoon, he looked back at her. As far as he could see, they were the only people out on this part of the lagoon.

"What do you want to do after we get back to the hut?" he called over his shoulder.

"I'd love to go to that coral sea garden and do some more snorkeling."

"That makes two of us. When in our lives will we ever have a chance to see fish like this up close?"

"Probably never. I'm still pinching myself to believe there's a spot like this on earth."

"We'll eat a meal and then go out for the rest of the day. Do you know what?"

"What?"

"You're more fun than any of my friends."

"Thank you."

"I mean it. I don't know anyone, male or female, who loves what I love and can do everything with me and keep up."

"I'm afraid I didn't turn out to be like my socialite parents."

"Thank heaven!"

Those two words warmed her heart all the way back to their island. After putting things away, they sat down to a meal, then went back out to the deck. Antonio covered her in sunscreen. His touch made her knees buckle. "Shall we stay in bed the rest of the day instead?"

Christina could hardly talk. "I'd love it, but our time here is so short, we need to take advantage of it." She couldn't believe she'd worried that in a week Antonio might be bored with her. Maybe it was because all the time they'd spent together in Switzerland had prepared her to be more comfortable with him where everything felt so natural.

"Just remember we'll have all night," he whispered against her neck. His breath sent tendrils of delight through her system. While she was still trying to recover, he got out the snorkels and fins. Once again they got into the boat and went looking for fish. The lagoon was home to so many species they had the time of their lives viewing everything.

She lost track of the time. So did Antonio. It wasn't until they suffered hunger pains that she realized it was time to go in. When they returned to the island and were tying up the boat, Manu was there to greet them.

"You two must have had a good day to be out so long."

Christina smiled at him. "Every day is a good day here." But she sensed he had something else on his mind. So did Antonio.

"What's wrong, Manu?"

"There was a call from the palace in Halencia. You are to call your sister as soon as you can. You can use the phone here and I'll put it through for you."

Both Christina and Antonio exchanged worried glances. Any number of things could be wrong for her to interrupt their honeymoon. "Thank you. I'll do it as soon as we're finished here."

"Your dinner is in the kitchen when you want to eat."

"You're terrific, Manu," she said.

After he disappeared, Antonio helped her out of the boat and they put their gear away. Already there was a change in her husband. Lines darkened his features, making him look older. They'd had an unforgettable night of loving and had been so carefree she could have cried to see that anxious look cross over his face.

Together they walked inside the bedroom of the hut, both of them still wearing their bathing suits. He turned to her. "I'm going to put on a robe, then make the call."

While he went into the bathroom to change, she pulled out some underwear and dressed in a pair of tan shorts and a cream top. Then she hung her bikini over the outside rail to dry, all the time frightened something serious had happened back home. An accident, or worse?

Antonio came out of the bathroom and walked over to the side of the bed to the phone. She sat down next to him. He put the phone on speaker and grasped her hand while he waited for Manu to connect the call.

"Tonio?"

"Elena?" His heart was racing. "What's wrong?"

"I'm so sorry to bother you on your honeymoon, but—"

"Is anyone ill?"

"No, no. Everyone's fine, but there's something you need to know. I hope you're sitting down to hear this."

Antonio looked at his wife, anxious for what was coming. "Go ahead."

"I—I have to give you some background first," she stammered. "You know that guy Rolfe? The drug addict I wish I'd never met?"

He sucked in his breath. "Yes?"

"Last week he was arrested on heavier drug charges. He called me from the jail and told me that if I didn't help him out of the new charges, he'd tell the press everything about what happened when he was jailed the first time."

"What?" he and Christina cried out at the same time. His thoughts were reeling.

"I thought he was high on drugs when he called me and I hung up on him. But he phoned me on the morning you were getting married and threatened me again. I told him there wasn't anything I could do. He hung up on me telling me I'd be sorry.

"Oh, Tonio—he leaked the news about your fake engagement to the press. It's all over the media that you thought up the bogus alliance with Christina to get me out of trouble with the police. He claimed I used drugs too and should have been jailed along with him.

"It's gone viral too. The internet is alive with rumours that you were having an affair in California while Christina was in Africa having an affair with the doctor. He made it all up, but it's done its damage.

"Marusha phoned me and told me she and her family are sick about this and want to know what they can do to stop it getting any worse. I don't know what to do.

"The palace is in an uproar. Both sets of parents are beside themselves. Guido's trying to help everything by preparing a new list of princesses. In case you can somehow salvage your reputation and get your marriage annulled, you'll have a list of royal hopefuls to choose from. I'm fighting for you, Tonio, but I can't do it alone."

Pain ripped him apart. His arm went around

his wife. He could only imagine how Christina was feeling right now.

"I heard Father give immediate orders for the jet to be flown to Tahiti to bring you home. It's on its way now and will arrive at the airport at six in the morning Tahitian time. You need to be ready with a plan and come home as quickly as you can to help sort out this disaster, because that's what it is!

"There's a groundswell from people who don't believe you should be crowned because of the lie. I've been labeled a drug addict and am the result of my parents who aren't worthy of ruling the country. The people are afraid the lack of integrity on both your part and Christina's has compromised everything.

"If feelings reach tipping point, the people could withdraw their support for the monarchy and this could be the end of it. The coronation has been called off until further notice."

"No," Christina cried out.

"Oh, Christina, I didn't know you were listening. Let's face it. I'm the one responsible for all this. I'm the reason any of this has happened and I feel so horrible about it

I want to die. I never realized how vindictive Rolfe could be. How cruel and heartless after what you did to get him a light sentence. I spent time with him when I was at my most rebellious and wasn't careful with the information I let out without realizing it. You and Christina have every right to hate me."

"Of course we don't hate you," he ground out. "For now you'll just have to hang on until we get back to Halencia. Trust me. We're going to sort this out. I'll talk to you tomorrow in person. And, Elena, never forget that we love you."

Christina had buried her face in her hands. *"Bellissima—"* He took her in his arms.

Hearing that word applied to her produced a groan from her. She was so horrified over the news she felt physically ill and couldn't form words.

His body stiffened. "I wondered what form of chicanery has been underfoot while we were on our honeymoon. It's what I expected. I just didn't know in the exact manner it would explode. Christina? Look at me."

She tried, but his image was blurry.

"I know this has come as a shock, but we're

going to get through this because there's been total honesty between us, *grazie a Dio*. Remember Elena needs our protection more than ever. She's very fragile right now."

"You're right. I knew there was something wrong when she kept saying she hoped we'd be happy. Throughout our wedding she was terrified and had to keep all that bottled up inside. The poor thing."

He kissed her lips. "I'll make arrangements for the helicopter to be here at five a.m. Then you and I are going to have a long, serious talk."

His composure under these precarious circumstances was nothing short of miraculous. The affairs of the kingdom were falling apart, yet his mastery in dealing with it was a revelation. As far as she was concerned, this was Antonio's finest hour.

Whether she ever became queen or not, she would act like one right now because Antonio had never needed her help more to present a unified front. She knew deep down he wanted to be king in order to save his country from possible ruin. More than anything, Christina wanted that for him, whatever it took.

She grabbed two bottles of water from the refrigerator and hurried through the hut to their bedroom. While she waited for him to come, she started the packing for both of them. Five o'clock would be here soon enough. They needed to be ready to leave.

Christina lifted her head when he came into the bedroom with their dinner tray. "Did you get through to Manu?"

He nodded. "Everything is set. Since you've packed the bags, we can eat." He put it on the bed. "Come on."

She took a shaky breath. "I—I couldn't."

"You have to. I don't want my wife getting sick on me. We're on our honeymoon and I intend to enjoy it for the next six hours."

Christina actually laughed despite her agony.

Together they got on the bed and ate. When they'd finished eating, he got up to put the tray on the table. "Excuse me a moment. I'll be right back."

She wondered what he was doing until she heard Tahitian music from the radio piped into their room. Once he reappeared, he turned off the lamps and crawled onto the bed beside her.

"This music is enchanting, isn't it?" she said.

"I love it. Come here to me," he whispered. "I need you."

The blood pounded in her ears before she moved into his arms. "What are we going to do, Antonio?"

"We're going to stay just like this."

"You know what I mean."

"Yes, but there's nothing to do about anything until we reach Halenica, so you're stuck with me."

"That's no penance. You smell wonderful."

"So you've noticed."

She swallowed hard. "I notice everything."

"So do I. You're a warrior under that fiery mane."

"What a compliment."

"It is, because you're going to be queen and now I know you have the steel to help me. Any other woman would have gone into hysterics a little while ago. Not you."

She smiled in secret pleasure. "You wouldn't let me. That's the sign of a great king."

"The priest's words never had as much meaning to me until now."

"Which words were those?"

"The part where he said 'From this day

forward you shall be each other's home, comfort and refuge.' Whatever we have to face when we get back home, Christina, I'm not worried because you've become my refuge in a very short time."

Tears stung her eyelids. He kissed them. "I didn't mean to make you cry."

"It's the good kind. When I'm happy, I often cry."

"I saw tears when you looked at your parents in the chapel. What was going on in your mind?"

"That I didn't always want to be a disappointment to them. Now that there's a national scandal, they'll consider that I've hit rock bottom."

"If they can't see beyond the end of their noses and recognize a hatchet job of major proportions, how sad for them. But I couldn't be happier that you turned out just the way you are. My one regret is that we're going to have to leave our paradise far too soon. I've had you all to myself since the wedding ceremony and I love the privacy so much I'm loath to give it up."

"I feel the same. We've been living most people's fantasy."

He suddenly held her tighter and burrowed his face in her neck. "I want this fantasy to go on and on." The longing in his voice echoed the desire of her heart. "I want you to know I'll treasure this time together for the rest of my life."

"I've loved every second of it too. Isn't this place wonderful?"

"Yes, but it would be a waste without the right person along. We'll come back again one day and spend time over at the coral garden. We'll do a lot of things, but right now I just want to make love to you."

Once again the age-old ritual began. This time Christina took the initiative to show her husband how much she loved him. She loved him in every atom of her body and poured out her feelings, wanting to take away any pain he was feeling tonight. At one point he pulled her on top of him. It was heaven to cover his face with kisses and play with his hair. He was such a beautiful man, there were no words.

"Christina? We only have a few hours before we have to return to Halencia and deal with the mess. If I'd known it was going to happen, I would have insisted we get married sooner and enjoy a month's honeymoon at least. Now it's too late for that."

But before their wedding, neither of them had a clue that they would come to care for each other in so short a time. Christina was positive that flare of desire she'd felt when he kissed her at the altar had been unexpected for him too.

"Are you happy?" His voice sounded anxious. "Because I want you to be happy."

She heard the longing and drew in a breath. "I'm happier right now than I've ever been in my life."

"*Grazie a Dio*, because I am too. I hope our daughter has red hair like her mother."

"Would you mind if our son has red hair instead?"

"Your hair is glorious. Why would I mind?"

"Mother wanted to turn me into a brunette."

"It's a good thing you didn't listen to her. When the time came, I wanted you for my bride."

Yes. And he wound up with Christina to save his sister from disgrace. And now that the news had leaked, it was a national scandal, but he didn't seem worried.

Their trust was on solid ground. More than ever she understood the deeper words of the priest. *Be able to forgive, do not hold grudges, and live each day that you may share it together. From this day forward you shall be each other's home, comfort and refuge, your marriage strengthened by your love and respect.*

So far they'd shared each incredible day together. Their nights had been euphoric. This bedroom had become their home and refuge. She'd been able to comfort him in a way she wouldn't have imagined. Living with Antonio was already changing her life and it frightened her that the happiness she was experiencing might be taken away from her after they returned home.

The next morning they awakened for breakfast. It had arrived with a newspaper. He pored over it.

Her heart thudded. "Anything to report about us?"

"There's a photo of me taken at the airport. No matter how hard my father tried, the word still got out. But so far Manu has managed to keep our exact location a secret. He's worth every Eurodollar he's being paid."

"Do you think your father will be upset?"

"Yes." He flicked her a searching glance. "Are you in with me?"

"All the way. You know that."

He put the newspaper down and moved himself away from the table. "Come out on the deck with me. I crave a walk along the beach with you before it rains."

Her husband reached for her hand as they stepped down to the edge of the water and started walking. "With Bora Bora appearing and disappearing mystically through the clouds this morning, it looks surreal, Antonio. I feel like we're in some primordial world. The air is so balmy it's unreal."

After they'd gone a ways, he stopped and grasped her arms so she faced him. "You're so lovely *you* seem unreal. I need to know if I'm with a phantom wife." In the next breath he lowered his mouth to hers and gave her the husband's kiss she'd been dying for. Fire licked through her veins as she was caught up in his embrace. She knew he had to be in pain, but the way he was kissing her had her senses reeling.

Their bodies clung. She could feel the powerful muscles in his legs and melted against him. He released her mouth long enough to kiss her face and neck. His hands plunged into her hair before he kissed her throat, in fact, all the area of skin exposed by the sundress she was wearing home.

"Touch me," he whispered in a ragged voice.

Succumbing to his entreaty, she wrapped her arms around his waist and heard his moan of pleasure as his mouth began devouring hers. The rain had started and was so ethereal in nature it felt more like a mist, adding to the rapture building inside her. Antonio was doing the most amazing things to her with his hands and mouth.

Too soon Manu arrived to tell them the helicopter had arrived. It was time to go.

CHAPTER EIGHT

THIRTY HOURS LATER the royal jet landed at Voti International Airport, where a helicopter was waiting to fly them to the palace. To their relief, no press was allowed on the tarmac.

During the times throughout the flight while Christina napped, Antonio had talked with his sister at length to get her to stop blaming herself. During the night his wife had been restless and couldn't sleep. They were flying home to a hornet's nest. She was holding her own, but he knew the emotions of his brave, beautiful wife were in turmoil.

At one o'clock that afternoon the helicopter landed on the back lawn of the palace closed to the public. He helped her down and they hurried toward the south entrance with several staff members bringing their luggage.

They rushed up the grand staircase to the second floor of the east wing. When he reached the doors of his apartment, he picked her up again like a bride.

"Antonio—" She hid her head against his shoulder. "We've already done this once."

"I don't care. I might feel like doing it every time we come in." Before she could say another word, he silenced her with a kiss because he couldn't help himself. She'd become the drug in his system. Her response electrified him. At this point he needed to be with her inside their home away from the world and make love to his wife.

After managing to open one of the two tall, palatial doors, he swept her through the apartment to the bedroom and followed her down on the bed. The staff knew better than to do anything but place the suitcases inside the main doors and leave them alone.

"Welcome to my world, Christina de L'Accardi. Besides family, you're the first and only woman I've ever brought here. It's always been a lonely place for me. Now it's going to be our home." It was liberating to crush her against him. One kiss turned into another. She wanted him as much as he wanted her.

Like clockwork both his cell phone and room phone started ringing. He moaned aloud before continuing to kiss her, but the ringing persisted until she tore her lips from his. "Of course everyone knows we're back, Antonio," she said out of breath. "You at least have to say hello."

"That's all I'll say." He sat up and reached for the bedside phone first, impatient because of the interruption of civilization. Being away from technology for a few days had been the best thing that could have happened to them. *"Pronto—"*

"Come sta, figlio mio?"

He looked at his wife, whose silvery eyes fastened on him still had the glaze of desire burning in their depths. His fingers ran over her lips. "Christina and I have been to heaven thanks to your generosity, Papa. But we were called back to earth too soon."

"I'm thrilled you've had a wonderful time, but now we must talk."

"Not now, Papa. My wife and I need the rest of this day together."

"But there's a crisis."

His muscles clenched. "So I've been informed, but nothing's more important than my time with her. I promise I'll take care of things starting tomorrow. Give my love to Mama. *Ciao.*"

Christina chuckled. "You'll have to answer your cell phone or it will never stop." Letting out another sound of frustration, he reached in his pants pocket and pulled it out. When he saw the caller ID, he didn't mind answering.

"Zach!"

"I'm glad you answered. Where are you?" His friend sounded more than anxious.

He smiled down at Christina. "We've just entered our humble home after being flown to paradise and back." She kissed his fingers.

"I've never thought of Paris as paradise."

"No. Bora Bora. A surprise wedding gift from my parents. You should take Lindsay there. You'd never want to come back."

"Antonio? Is this really you? You sound strange, like you're on something."

He grinned. "I've been drugged all right." A laugh came out of his wife. "Listen, I'll call you tomorrow."

"But you've got problems, buddy. Big problems."

"My other half is going to help me solve them."

"But she's part of the problem, if you get my meaning," Zach said, lowering his voice.

"You've got that wrong. She's the solution, but I appreciate your concern. You're the best friend a man ever had next to his wife. *Ciao*."

No sooner had he hung up to indulge himself with his beautiful bride than Christina's cell phone rang. She had to get off the bed for the purse she'd accidentally dropped on the inlaid wooden flooring while her husband was carrying her.

She didn't need to look at the caller ID to know who it was. Might as well get this over now. *"Pronto?"*

"Christina?" Her mother sounded mournful rather than angry. "Is it true that you had an affair while you were engaged to Antonio?"

She held her breath. "If I tell you that was a lie, would you believe me?"

"Yes."

"Would Father?"

"I—I can't speak for him. What are you going to do?"

Her mother sounded as though she really cared. "It's up to Antonio."

"Just remember I'm here for you if you need me."

For her mother to say that was astounding to Christina. "Thank you, Mama. We'll talk later."

Antonio's arms were locked around her from behind. But for once she didn't feel like crawling into a dark hole never to come out again. She turned to Antonio. "Mother just gave me her support."

"It's about time, but don't forget you've got me now."

"I know." She lifted her mouth to kiss him, but there was a knocking on the outer doors, loud enough to reach their ears in the bedroom. "Tonio? It's me," Elena cried. "Can I come in? It's an emergency!"

"Tell her to come," Christina urged him. "She's been waiting for us."

He gave her another hug before they both hurried through the apartment to greet his sister.

When he opened the door, they barely recognized Elena, who'd been crying for so long her blue eyes were puffy and her face had gone splotchy. "I'm so glad you're home." She threw herself into Antonio's arms and sobbed.

Christina closed the door and the three of them went into the living room. When he let her go, she turned to Christina. As they hugged, his sister had another explosion of tears.

"Elena—it's going to be all right. Come and sit down on the couch." She drew her by the hand. Antonio sat in the love seat near them.

She brushed the tears from her cheeks. "I have something to tell both of you. Marusha and I have had a long talk. Her husband found out through another doctor that before Roger left Africa, he got drunk and told things to the doctor that were supposed to be kept quiet. But the other doctor was unscrupulous and leaked it to the news."

Christina shook her head. "I should never have gone out with him."

Antonio stood up. "If we all keep blaming

ourselves for everything, nothing will be accomplished. What's done is done."

"There's more," Elena admitted.

He took a deep breath. "Go on."

"I broke down and told our parents why you and Christina got engaged. I also told them Christina had never slept with that doctor. It was pure fabrication."

"It's all right, Elena. The truth will free all of us."

His wife was so right!

He'd already known that Christina hadn't given herself to the doctor. Antonio had been stunned at the time and overjoyed.

"They think you're both so noble," Elena kept on. "Our parents are prepared to do anything to help you. But as you know, they've lost Guido's respect and he has powerful friends in the council who are ready to abolish the monarchy altogether. Some of the others wanting to keep the monarchy alive have prevailed on the archbishop to grant an annulment so you can remarry. There's a list of titled women they're vetting now with Princess Gemma at the top."

Filled with joy that Christina was his wife,

Antonio stopped pacing. "No. That isn't going to happen. I've got plans, ideas to build the economy. Christina and I plan to enlarge the African charity to make it far-reaching. I have a new jobs initiative to help us become a leader in technology. Scandal has rocked this nation for years, but we'll weather it. We have to."

Elena stared at him as if she'd never seen him before.

His wife got up from the couch and stood in front of him, wearing the same white suit she'd worn on the plane to Tahiti. *"We will."*

Two beautiful words from the mouth of the woman he couldn't imagine living without. He kissed her in front of his sister before walking over to Elena and pulling her to her feet. "I'm glad the truth is out, all of it." He gave her a hug. "Everything is going to work out."

"It's got to, because I love you two so much."

Antonio looked at his clever, adorable wife. She was so remarkable he couldn't believe he was lucky enough to be married to her.

He brushed his sister's cheek with his finger. "So, what is the latest between you and Enzio?"

"We're good."

"Just good."

"Um, very good."

"I'm glad to hear it."

"But you don't need to hear about my love life right now. I'm going to leave you to your privacy and will talk to you later."

They both hugged her before she hurried out of the apartment. He put his arm around Christina's waist and walked her back to the bedroom. "Before we do anything else, I need to take another look at your foot. Why don't you get undressed first? I want to make certain it is healing properly."

"This is almost like déjà vu."

While she started to take off her top and pants, her phone rang again. She'd left it on the end of the bed. "Let me get this first." The caller ID said it was her great-aunt calling.

She clicked on. "Sofia?"

"Welcome home, darling. How was your trip?"

"Heavenly."

"But you've come home to a viper's nest. I know something that you don't and I'm calling to warn you."

Antonio came to stand next to her.

She gripped the phone harder. "What is it?"

"I've spent part of the day with your parents. Your father has left for the palace to talk to you. I tried in my own way to ask him to wait until tomorrow, but you know how he is."

Yes... Christina knew exactly.

"For once in your life, darling, stand up to him and don't let him bully you. He's like his father and grandfather, born mean-spirited."

This conversation meant her father was furious. "He's a hard man to confront because he doesn't have a soft side."

"Unfortunately your mother has always been too afraid of him to intercede for you."

Her eyes filmed over. "I always had you, Aunt Sofia."

"And you've been one of my greatest joys."

"Thank you for alerting me."

"If there's anything I can do..."

Christina turned to Antonio. "My husband and I are prepared to face whatever is coming. I love you so much for caring. Talk to you again soon." She clicked off.

"What's going on?" he murmured.

"My father is on his way over to talk to me."

"I won't leave you alone with him."

She loved Antonio for saying that. "Knowing his style of quick attack, he won't be here long. Do you mind if we talk in the living room?"

"Of course not. This is our home. You can have anyone you want here, anytime."

"Thank you." She rose on tiptoe and kissed him.

"I'll go downstairs to my office and talk to my executive assistant. If you need me, I'll be here in an instant." She nodded. He put on a fresh sport shirt and left the apartment. Antonio was far too handsome for his own good.

This was her first chance to walk around her new home. The palace was a magnificent structure. Antonio's apartment was bigger than any home she'd ever been in. Already she knew her favorite place would be the terrace overlooking the water.

To think Antonio had been born here and had lived here until he was old enough to be sent away to schools and college. There was so much to learn about him as a child as well as an adult, but she couldn't concentrate when she knew her father would be coming any minute.

The phone on the bedside table rang. She walked over to pick it up. "Yes?"

"Princess Christina? This is the office calling. Your father is here to speak to you."

"Can you send him to our apartment?"

"Si, signora."

"Grazie."

"Prego."

Five minutes later she heard the knock on the door and opened it to see her father standing there. "Come into the living room, Papa."

He looked around while he followed her, but he didn't take a seat when she suggested it.

"Where's your husband?"

"In his office downstairs."

"What I have to say won't take long."

It never does.

His eyes glittered with anger. "If you want to do one thing to restore the name Rose in people's estimation, you'll leave Antonio for the good of the monarchy."

"I thought you wanted a king for a son-in-law."

He stared at her. "Not when his queen dishonored him by being with another man during the engagement. The people will forgive him, but they'll never forgive you."

She lifted her chin. "I didn't dishonor him. Is that all you came to say?"

His lips thinned. "Use the one shred of decency left in you to allow Antonio to rule with the right queen at his side. He may stand by you now, but in time doubts will creep in, and doubt can ruin a marriage faster than anything else. Let him marry Princess Gemma."

"Antonio didn't want her the first time around. He chose me."

Her father's cheeks grew ruddy. "The archbishop will sanction a divorce since the marriage was fraudulent and your behavior during the engagement has painted you an immoral woman. You have one more opportunity in your life to right a tremendous wrong. Then public sentiment will end up being kind to you."

"So if I do that and bow out of his life, will you forgive me for being born a woman instead of a man and be kind to me?"

"The one has nothing to do with the other."

Her breath caught. "You mean that no matter what I do, there can be no forgiveness from you in this life?"

"You always were a difficult child."

She stiffened and fought her tears. "I'm your daughter. Yours and Mother's. I wanted your love. I wanted your acceptance. I tried everything under the sun to be the child you could love."

"We gave you everything, didn't we?" He turned to leave.

"Papa—"

Halfway out the door he said, "Has he told you he loves you? Because if he hasn't, then you need to do the right thing. If you don't know what is in Antonio's heart, why take the risk?"

Beyond tears, she walked out to the terrace, clutching her arms to her waist. The warning phone call from her aunt Sofia hadn't helped. She'd been thrown into a black void. Antonio had never said he loved her. She hadn't expected him to love her, but that was before they'd gone to Tahiti together and she'd found rapture with him.

If she truly didn't know what was in Antonio's heart, then was it a risk to stay in the marriage as her father said?

After standing there for a while, she went back to the bedroom and called the palace switchboard. "Would you connect me with the palace press secretary please?"

"*Si.*"

In a minute a male voice came on the line.

"This is Princess Christina. I have a statement to come out on the evening news. I'll have it sent to your office by messenger. If you value your job, you'll tell no one. I mean, not a single soul."

"*Capisco*, Princess."

She hung up and went into the den, where she wrote out what she wanted to say. It didn't take long. After putting the note in an envelope and sealing it, she phoned the charity foundation in Voti. Arianna, the manager, answered the phone. Thank heaven she was still there.

"Christina? I can't believe you're calling. I thought you were on your honeymoon."

"We're back. I need a favor from you. A big one. Can you stop what you're doing right now and drive to the west gate of the palace?"

"Well, yes."

"I'll be waiting. This is an emergency."

"I'll be there in five minutes."

"Bless you."

She hung up and started throwing the things she'd need for overnight in her large tote bag. There was always money in her bank account and she had her passport. Without stopping to think, she left the apartment and hurried down the long hall of the west wing to the staircase.

When she reached the main doors, she stopped to talk to one of the guards. "Would you see that the palace press secretary receives this immediately?"

"Of course."

"Thank you."

Then she passed through the doors to the outside where another guard was on duty. "If the prince wonders where I am, tell him that an emergency came up at the charity foundation in town. One of my head people is picking me up so we can deal with it. I'll phone the prince later, but he's in meetings right now and can't be disturbed."

"*Capisco.*"

So far, so good. She rushed outside and waited under the portico until she saw Arianna's red Fiat. Christiana hurried around the passenger side and got in. "You are an angel, Arianna, and I'll give you a giant bonus."

"Where do you want to go?"

"Back to the foundation." She put on her sunglasses. It only took a few minutes to reach the building. "Why don't you go on home? I'll be working late and will lock up again."

"All right."

"This is for your trouble." She handed her a hundred Eurodollars and got out of the car. When her friend drove off smiling, Christina hailed a taxi and asked to be driven to the ferry terminal. There were ferries leaving on the hour for Genoa during the summer.

She paid the driver, then hurried inside and bought a ticket. Within twenty minutes she walked onto the ferry and sat on a bench as it made its way to the port in Genoa. From there she transferred to the train station and caught the next train going to Monte Calanetti via Siena. So far no one had recognized her because pictures of her wedding to Antonio hadn't been given to the press.

When it pulled in to the station, she phoned Louisa.

"Dear friend?" she said when Louisa answered.

"Christina?"

"Yes. I'm in Monte Calanetti. Do you have room for a visitor?"

"Did I just hear you correctly?"

"Yes."

"Of course I have room!" No doubt Louisa figured correctly that there'd been trouble since their flight back from Tahiti. "You can stay in the bridal suite for as long as you want."

"Thank you from the bottom of my heart. I'll be there soon and tell you everything."

As the taxi drove her to the Palazzo di Comparino, she turned off her phone. No one knew where she'd gone and that was the way she wanted things to stay.

Antonio had spent more time in his office than he'd meant to. He'd given Christina as much time as she needed to be with her father. After taking care of some business matters, he hurried to his wing of the palace. He planned to order a special dinner for them and eat out on the terrace. Having to come home early had robbed them of another precious night in Bora Bora, but tonight he intended to make up for everything. The need to make love to his wife was all he could think about.

"Christina?" There was no answer. He walked through to their bedroom. She wasn't there. Maybe she'd gone exploring, but she hadn't left a note. It was possible that after being with her father she'd gone to visit Elena. He phoned his sister. "Does Christina happen to be with you?"

"No."

"Hmm. I was doing a little business, but she's not here."

"She loves the outdoors. Maybe she took a walk outside to the kennel. That's what we usually do when she visits me. You know how much she adores animals."

"Thanks for the tip."

He put through a call to the kennel, but no one had seen her.

Angry with himself for not putting a security detail on her first thing, he phoned the head of palace security. "Alonzo? I'm looking for Princess Christina. Find out where she is and let me know ASAP. I want surveillance on her twenty-four-seven starting now."

"Yes, Your Highness."

He put off ordering dinner and hurried downstairs to the palace's main office. "Did anyone here see Princess Christina's father arrive?"

One of them nodded. "The princess asked that he be shown to your apartment. About twenty minutes later he passed by the office and left the grounds in a limousine."

More than frustrated at this point, Antonio headed for Alonzo's office. "Any news about her yet?"

Alonzo shook his head. "We're still vetting everyone on the force. Some of them went off shift at five o'clock and we're still trying to reach them for information."

He frowned. She wouldn't have gone to his parents' apartment, would she? He called them on the chance that she was there for some reason. But they had nothing to tell him.

Definitely worried now, he put through a call to Christina's parents. He should have tried there first. Her father got on the other extension. "Your Highness?"

"I'm looking for my wife. If you have any idea where she is, I'd like you to tell me now. The last anyone saw of her was you."

"You mean she's missing?"

His anger was approaching flash point. "What did you say to her?"

"The only thing a good father could say to his daughter. Do the right thing."

Antonio saw red. He clicked off and spun around in fury. It was almost nine o'clock. Could she have flown to Nairobi without telling him?

Frantic, he asked Alonzo for his men to check the airport to see if she'd flown out. Within a few minutes the news came back that she hadn't boarded any planes going anywhere.

"Hold on, Antonio. There's another report coming in. The guard at the west gate saw her leave the palace grounds in a red Fiat before he went off duty just before five. He had no idea you were looking for her. She told him she was going to the charity foundation to take care of an emergency and didn't want you to worry."

His hands balled into fists. "Find out if she's still there! We need to call all the girls working there to find out who drove the Fiat."

Before long the report came back that the building was closed for the night. No sign of Princess Christina anywhere. In another minute they had a woman on the line. Antonio took the call. "Arianna?"

"Your Highness. I didn't realize you were looking for her. When I dropped her off in front of the building, she said she was going to work in there for a while and that I should go home."

"So you have no idea where she went, or if she even went inside."

"No. I'm so sorry."

"What state was she in?"

"She definitely had an agenda and asked me to hurry, but that's all."

"Thank you, Arianna."

He handed the phone back to Alonzo.

Where are you, Christina. What did your father say to turn you inside out?

While he stayed there in agony, wondering where to turn next, the press secretary, Alonzo, came hurrying into the office. "Your Highness?"

Antonio turned to him. "Do you have news about the princess?"

His face had gone white. "I do. She told me if I said anything I'd lose my job, but I can't let you suffer like this."

"What do you know?"

"She handed me an envelope and wanted the television anchor to read her statement during the ten o'clock news."

"She *what*?"

He nodded. "It'll be on every network in five minutes in every country in the world."

Alonzo turned on the big-screen television in his office. Antonio felt so gutted he started to weave.

"Better sit down, Your Highness."

"I'll be all right." His heart plummeted to his feet as he saw the words *breaking news* flash across the screen.

Suddenly the female news anchor appeared. "There's huge news breaking from the royal palace in Voti, Halencia, tonight, threatening to rock the already shaky monarchy decimated by scandal. It is struggling to stay alive in a nation so divided that one wonders what the ultimate outcome will be.

"I have in front of me a statement that Princess Christina, recently married in a private ceremony to Crown Prince Antonio de L'Accardi, has asked the press to read. These are her words and I quote. 'Dear citizens of Halencia. It is with the greatest sadness that I, Princess Christina de L'Accardi, am removing myself from the royal family to end the bitter conflict. I confess that although my relationship with Prince Antonio started out as a publicity stunt for reasons I don't intend to go into, I want everyone to know I love my new husband with every fiber of my being. A man with his integrity doesn't come along every day, or even in a lifetime. I knew him when we were both teenagers. Even then he showed a love and loyalty to his country that put others to shame. I want everyone to know he's the light of my life and my one true love. But I'm sorry that it isn't enough for the people of Halencia.'"

Christina...his heart cried.

"Wow! How's that for a heartfelt confession from the 'Cinderella Bride' as the nation has called her? Her charity in Africa has gained international attention. I have to admit I'm moved by her sacrifice and graciousness. That doesn't happen to me very often. Stay tuned for news coming from the palace as the fallout from her surprising statement is felt throughout the country and the world.

"There's no word from the prince or his family about this shocking development. You'll have to stayed tuned when more news will be forthcoming."

The television was shut off. Alonzo eyed Antonio with concern. "We'll find her. Just give us time."

"Thank you, Alonzo." But he knew the damage had been done when her father talked to her. He'd done such an expert job of destroying her that Antonio doubted Christina might ever come out of hiding.

As he left the office and started up the staircase for his apartment on legs that felt like lead, his phone started ringing. He looked down. Good old faithful Zach. He clicked on.

"Antonio?"

"*Si?*"

"What a hell of a mess."

"That doesn't even begin to cover it," he half groaned.

CHAPTER NINE

September, Voti, Halencia

AFTER HIS SPEECH, Antonio stood before the divided government assembly to answer questions.

"With all due respect, Your Highness, Princess Christina has graciously stepped aside to appease those voices who still want you to rule, but with someone more befitting to be your consort. Why won't you listen to reason?"

His anger was acute. "What princess on your short list has devoted half her life to charity and worked among the poverty-stricken in Africa with no thought for herself? What princess would willingly give up the title of queen in order not to stand in the way of her husband?"

The room grew quiet.

"My wife hasn't made excuses or defended herself, so I'll do it for her. This so-called affair of hers was in truth a friendship, nothing more, but trust evil to find its way to do its dirty work. She remained true to our engagement. So I'll say it again. If I can't rule with Christina at my side, then I have no desire to rule. Therefore I've given orders that there'll be no coronation."

A loud roar of dissent from that part of the council loyal to him and the crown got to their feet, but he was deaf to their cries.

"But, Your Highness—"

Antonio ignored the minister of finance, his good friend, who was calling to him and stormed out of the council meeting. He walked out of chambers and headed straight for his office down the hall of the palace.

"Roberto?" he barked.

"Your Highness?" His assistant's head came up.

"Call the press secretary and ask him to come in here right away. No one is to disturb us, do you understand?"

"*Si.*" He picked up the phone immediately.

Antonio went into his private suite and slammed the door, but he was too full of adrenaline to sit. With Christina's stunning press statement read over the airwaves three weeks ago, plus her disappearance that had come close to destroying him, the joy he'd experienced on his honeymoon had vanished. He felt as if he'd been shoved down a pit and was falling deeper and deeper with no end in sight.

Within a few hours of searching for her that night, Alonzo's security people had tracked his wife to the Palazzo di Comparino. Apparently Louisa had taken her in. His clever, resourceful wife had made her getaway so fast by car, taxi, ferry and train that it had knocked the foundation from under him.

There'd been no word from her for the past desolate three weeks, but he hadn't expected any. Her father had made certain of that. With her press statement ringing out over the land, she would never come to him now. Meanwhile, Antonio had made a firm decision. He'd meant what he'd just said before the council. If he didn't have her at his side, he didn't want to be king at all.

For the first time in his life he was doing what he wanted, and he wanted Christina. No amount of argument could persuade him to change his mind. Being reminded by Guido that Christina had decided to sacrifice her own heart for Antonio's reputation and the country had only made him fall harder for his wife, if that was possible.

Roberto buzzed him that the press secretary was outside. Antonio told him to send him in.

When the other man entered the room looking sheepish, Antonio said, "Do you want to redeem yourself?"

"Anything, Your Highness."

"I want you to arrange a press conference for me on the steps of the palace in approximately one hour."

"I'll do it at once, Your Highness."

Louisa had turned the sitting room at the palazzo into a TV room. Christina was grateful, since it was the only way she got information from the outside world. The rest of the times she took long walks and coordinated charity business with the foundations in both Halencia and Nairobi.

Between Marusha and Elena, she was kept apprised of their news. Marusha was pregnant after suffering two miscarriages. Christina couldn't be happier for her. Elena's boyfriend, Enzio, wanted to marry her, but it meant talking to her parents first and she was nervous about that.

Though there was plenty of talk because Louisa had constant visitors, no one mentioned Antonio in her presence. Her aching heart couldn't have handled talking about him. Marusha begged her to come back to Africa. She would always have a home waiting. Christina told her she'd be coming in a few days. She'd outstayed her welcome with Louisa. It was time to go.

This afternoon both love-smitten Daniella and Marianna had come over for an evening with the girls. Christina had the suspicion Louisa was trying to cheer her up. She loved her for it and it was fun for all of them to get together.

Louisa poured wine from the vineyard and showed off her expertise about the vintage. Christina was impressed that she knew so much about it. Nico definitely had something to do with it.

Dinner wouldn't be for another couple of hours. Christina wasn't a wine drinker, but this afternoon was special, so she joined in with the others to take a sip.

Marianna smiled. "Hey, you guys—want to know a little gossip? I overheard Connor and Isabella talking wedding plans with Lindsay."

"I knew it!" Louisa said while everyone cheered. "Oh—it's time for the six o'clock news."

"Do we care?" Daniella interjected.

"I do," Louisa exclaimed. She hurried over to the TV and turned it on. Christina was secretly glad, since it was the only way she had of knowing what was going on at the palace. Her heart was broken for Antonio, who was having to carry on through the fight to determine the destiny of his country.

"*Buonasera.* Tonight we have more breaking news coming from the royal palace in Voti, Halencia. Crown Prince Antonio de L'Accardi has broken his long silence and has prepared a statement, which we will bring to you from the front steps of the royal palace."

The image flashed to a somber Antonio

in a dark blue suit who was so gorgeous that Christina feared her heart would give out. The girls grew quiet as all eyes were focused on him.

"Fellow countrymen and women, these have been dark times for the crown and it's time for the conflict to end. I'll be brief. As I told the National Council this morning, I dare any tabloid to come after me or my wife again."

What? Christina shot to her feet.

"I admit that our engagement was originally a strategic move, but having spent time with Christina, I realize what an amazing person she is, how kind, generous and charitable she is, and how lucky this country is to have her as queen! I defy anyone to call our marriage a fake. To me it's the most real and true relationship I've ever had. So I'll tell you what I told the council. I'm in love with my wife and will *not* be giving her up, even if it means losing the throne!"

Christina was shaking so hard she might have fallen if she'd hadn't been holding on to the chair. The girls stared at her in wonder.

Louisa smiled at her. "Every woman in the

world with eyes in her head would love to be in your shoes right now, Christina Rose."

She nodded. "I'd like to be in them too, but he's not here."

Footsteps coming from the hall caused them to turn. Christina came close to fainting when Antonio walked in. "Who says I'm not?"

"Antonio," she gasped. "But you were just on television." He was dressed in a sport shirt and chinos instead of his dark suit.

"That was taped at noon. This afternoon the council reassembled and voted unanimously for our marriage to stand. The coronation will take place in two weeks. Once I was given the news, I flew here in the helicopter. It's standing by for me to take you back to the palace."

By now the girls were on their feet, hugging her and each other for joy.

Christina watched as her husband in all his male glory walked over to her. His brilliant blue eyes blinded her with their heat.

"H-how did you know I was here?"

"Palace security traced you once we heard from the guard that you'd left the grounds with Arianna."

"I thought I was being so careful."

"You were. For a few hours your disappearance gave me a heart attack. Since we'd barely returned from Bora Bora, I hardly think that's fair. Don't you ever do that to me again."

Her love for him was bursting out of her. "I promise."

In front of everyone he picked her up in his arms as he'd done twice before. "Excuse us, ladies. We have very personal matters of state to discuss and must get back to the palace. The limo is waiting for us."

Heat flooded her body as he carried her out of the room and the palazzo. After helping her into the car, he told the driver to head for Monte Calanetti before crushing her in his arms. "You don't have to worry about the state of our marriage, *cara*. I'm madly in love with you and this is a new day."

Christina was euphoric during their flight to Voti. Once they touched ground and were driven to the palace, he swept her along to their home on the second floor. Again he gathered her in his arms and carried her through to their bedroom.

After following her down onto the bed, he

began kissing her. They were starving for each other. Christina couldn't get enough of him fast enough. Everything that had kept them apart had been cleared away. She was able to give him all the love she'd stored up in her heart and body.

The next morning she heard a sound of satisfaction as he pulled her on top of him. Their night of lovemaking had appeased them for a little while. She sat up and looked at their clothes strewn all over the floor.

Antonio pulled her back down. "I'm in love with you, Christina. So terribly in love with my red-haired beauty I'll never get over it. You believe me, don't you?"

There was a vulnerability about the question that touched her heart. "I feel your love in every atom of my body, my darling. Is there any doubt how I feel about you after last night? I need you desperately and want your baby."

"Anything to oblige the woman who has made me thankful I was born a man."

"I loved you from the time I was fifteen, but I never dared admit it to myself because—"

Another kiss stifled any words. "We're never going to talk about past sadness. When

I called your father to find out what he said to you, he gave me the answer and I had a revelation of what it was like to grow up with him. All we can do is feel sorry for him. I believe your mother has always been afraid of him."

"I know you're right." Just when Christina didn't think she could love him anymore, he said or did something that made her love for him burn hotter. "I can't wait to thank your parents for Bora Bora."

"They've always lived their life over-the-top, but there's one thing they did I'll always be thankful for. They wanted us to find love."

"Yes, darling, and we found it there."

He kissed her neck and shoulders. "I'm the happiest man alive."

"Are you ready for a little more happy news?"

"What?"

"Enzio has asked Elena to marry him."

Antonio grinned. "He's a brave man to want to take her on."

"She's worth the risk. Guess what else? Marusha is expecting a baby." Christina kissed every feature. "I can't wait until we can announce we're having our own baby."

"I'm going to do my best to make that happen. I know now the one thing missing in my life was you and the family we're planning to have. We should have gotten married instead of engaged."

"I think about that too, all the time. But I don't think we were destined to get together until the time was right. We both had work to do first."

Antonio rolled her over and looked down at her. "You're the most beautiful sight this man has ever seen. I love you, *tesoro mio*. Never leave me."

"You *know* why I did."

A pained look entered his eyes. "The last three weeks have been the worst of my entire life."

"For me too. But as you said, no concentrating on past sorrows. We're together now and I'm able to live every day and night with the prince of my heart."

While they were talking, the house phone rang. She eyed her husband. "That's probably Guido wanting to know when you're free to discuss royal business. You better put him out of his misery."

Antonio grinned and picked up. *"Pronto."*

"Your Highness, Princess Christina's mother is asking if she can talk to her daughter in private."

He covered the mouthpiece. "Christina?" Curious, she looked at him. He stared into her eyes with concern. "Your mother wants to talk to you."

She swallowed nervously. "Is she on the phone?"

"No. It's Guido. What do you want to do?"

"I'll take the call."

He handed her the receiver. "Guido?"

"Your mother asks if she can come to your apartment to talk to you."

She blinked. "Now?"

"She's says it's of vital importance."

"Then have someone show her up."

"Very well."

Antonio had picked up on the conversation. "Are you sure you want to do this?"

"Yes. My mother let me know she's on our side. Why don't you order breakfast while I talk to her in the living room? She won't be here very long, no matter what is on her mind."

He pressed a swift kiss to her lips and did her bidding. As for herself, Christina could have changed into an outfit, but she decided the robe was perfectly presentable. Before long she heard a knock on the main door.

Sucking in her breath, she opened it. Her mother always looked impeccably dressed and coiffed. But Christina knew right away something was wrong when she saw the tears in her eyes. "Come in."

But she just stood there.

"Mother?"

She shook her head. "I thought I could do this, but I can't." She started to turn away.

"Can't do what?" Christina asked, causing her mother to stop.

"Ask your forgiveness, but I don't have the right. I lost the right years ago. I knew your father must have had emotional problems when you were born. He wanted to give you up for adoption because you weren't a boy. I purposely prevented any more pregnancies in case I had another girl."

Christina was aghast at what she was hearing, but it made sense when she considered what her great-aunt Sofia had told her about the Rose men.

"I bargained with him that I wanted to keep you, and he wouldn't be sorry. That's why I kept you away. But you'll never know my shame for what I've done." She hung her head.

"I may have given birth to you, and your father may have provided you with everything, but you didn't have parents who showed you the love and devotion you deserved."

Christina stood there in shock as her mother broke down and sobbed.

"I'll never be forgiven for what I did to you. I don't deserve forgiveness, but you're my sweet, darling girl. I love you, Christina. My pride in you is fierce. Just know that I loved you from the moment you were born and I wanted you to hear it from me. I won't bother you again."

"Mother? Don't say that. I want us to have the relationship we never had. It's never too late," Christina said in a tremulous voice. "What you've told me about Papa changes everything."

Her mother turned to her with a face glistening in tears. "You mean you don't hate me with every fiber of your being? I would, because I'm not the great person you are."

"Oh, Mama—"

Christina reached for her and hugged her until her mother reciprocated. They clung for a long time. With every tear her mother shed, Christina felt herself healing. "We'll invite you over for dinner in a few weeks. I'll be cooking." She kissed her mother on both cheeks. "Dry your tears and I'll see you soon."

"Bless you, *figlia mia*."

On Coronation Day bells rang out through the whole of Voti as Antonio and Christina left the cathedral and climbed into the open carriage. The massive throng roared, "Long live King Antonio and Queen Christina! Long live the monarchy!" They chanted the words over and over as the horses drew the carriage through the street lined with cheering Halencians.

The day had turned out to be glorious. Christina thought her heart was going to burst with happiness. Every few minutes someone called out, "Queen Christina!" When she turned, people were taking pictures.

Antonio sat next to her and squeezed the

hand that wasn't waving. "You know what they want, *bellissima*."

She looked back at him. "You mean a kiss? I want it much more." Showing breath-taking initiative that would probably cause her to blush later, she kissed him several times to the joy of the crowds.

The capital city of Halencia teemed with joyful faces and shouts of "Long live the monarchy."

"Your country loves you, darling. You don't know how magnificent you looked when the archbishop put that crown on your head."

"It's a good thing I didn't have to keep wearing it. How does yours feel?"

"I like the tiara. It's light."

"Your hair outshines its gleam."

They were both wearing their wedding clothes. The only thing different was the red sash on Antonio proclaiming him king.

"We made a lot of promises today." She kept waving. So did he.

"Are you worried?"

"No, but the sun is hot," he muttered. Their procession went on for over an hour.

Christina laughed. "I feel it too. But don't

worry. We'll make it through and be alone later."

"I can't wait."

Eventually the carriage returned them to the palace. On their way up to the balcony off the second floor, Antonio summoned Guido to bring them a sandwich and a drink. The chief of staff, who'd chosen to stay on with Antonio, looked shocked, but he sent someone for the food.

Antonio whispered in her ear, "Did you see that look he gave us?"

"We're breaking royal protocol, darling."

"We'll be breaking a lot of rules before my reign has come to an end."

She shivered. "Don't talk about that. I can't bear the thought of it."

When the sandwich arrived, they both ate a half and swallowed some water. Feeling slightly more refreshed, they walked out onto the balcony to the roar of the crowd.

To please them her husband kissed her again with so much enthusiasm she actually swayed in his arms. A thunderous roar of satisfaction broke from the enormous throng that filled every square inch of space.

Once the royal photographers had finished

taking pictures, Antonio grasped her hand. "Come with me."

"Where are we going?"

"To our home for some R and R until the ball this evening."

"But we're supposed to mingle with all the dignitaries."

"There'll be time for that tonight."

She hurried along with him, out of breath by the time they reached their apartment. When they entered, they discovered a lavish meal laid out for them in the dining room.

"Who arranged for this, darling?" she asked.

"My mother. She said it would be an exhausting day and we'd need it."

"I think she's wonderful."

Once in the bedroom, she removed her tiara and asked him to undo the buttons of her wedding dress. "That didn't take long. You did that so fast I'm afraid you've lost interest already. Last time you took forever."

"I hope it drove you crazy." He bit her earlobe gently when he'd finished. "Did it?"

"I'll never tell."

Antonio caught her to him and rocked her in his arms for a long, long time.

"Your capacity to love is a gift," he whispered against her cheek. "I don't know how I was the one man on earth lucky enough to be loved by you. I'm thankful your mother came to see you on the day we got back from Tuscany. She was able to answer the question that's always been in your heart. The sadness in your eyes has disappeared."

Christina threw her arms around his neck and looked into those blue eyes filled with love for her. "You're right. And now I have one more secret to disclose. You were always the man for me. When you asked me to get engaged, I jumped, *leaped* at the opportunity. To be honest, deep down I was petrified you *would* come to Africa and call it off. So I played it cagey, and it paid off!"

After enjoying a meal, they made love again before it was time to go out to greet their guests and enjoy the royal celebration. Guido looked frantic as they approached the balcony.

"Your Highness, we've been waiting for your appearance to start the fireworks."

Antonio hugged her waist. "We're here now."

No sooner had they stepped out so everyone could see them than a huge roar of excitement from the throng of people filled the air. Suddenly there was a massive fireworks display that lit up the sky, bursting and bursting, illuminating everything. Antonio looked into Christina's eyes. Her heart was bursting with happiness.

"Ti amo, Antonio."

He stared at her. "Darling, you're crying. What's wrong?"

"I'm so happy tonight I can't contain it all."

Giving the crowd what they wanted by kissing her, he whispered, "My beautiful wife. This is only the beginning. *Ti amo, bellissima.* Forever."

* * * * *